The World Within

By

Genie Euart

ISBN: 0-7596-8340-9

This book is printed on acid free paper.

1stBooks – rev. 12/14/01

THE LEGEND

In the predawn of history, when MAN first walked upon the earth, there was a race of wizards who ruled the land. Their powers were awesome, but their hand was cruel... And their god was Balim, the prince of darkness.

With their great powers and their mighty machines, they laid waste to the land and struck fear in the hearts of the people, and the people were much afraid, and there was none among them who could stand against this evil.

Seeing their suffering and the abuses wrought upon them, Yasha, the prince of light, raised up his hand. "Enough," he said. "My people have endured enough." And he sent Mikael, his servant, to smite the evil ones.

Mikael, with his legions, visited the will of Yasha upon Balim, the prince of darkness, and his evil followers. They struck the mighty waters with the sword of vengeance and created a giant maelstrom which swallowed up the land and all the followers of Balim and drew them down ... down into

THE WORLD WITHIN

PROLOGUE

Naila strode purposefully into her father's study. One tiny honey-gold curl had slipped from her perfectly coifed hair and she impatiently shook her head and directed a little stream of air in its direction to no avail. Finally, she pushed it back with her finger and, in so doing, dislodged her tiara slightly which exasperated her all the more. A definite frown crossed her brow.

"Father." It sounded more like an expletive than the usual endearing term with which she addressed her parent. She attempted to correct her error, for she truly loved her father; however, D'Ar raised a hand to silence her until he finished his writing, then looked up at his eldest daughter in open admiration. Maora would have been proud to see what a beautiful woman Naila had become.

"Father," she began again, somewhat softer than before, "something must be done about Leila." Her combined anger and frustration clearly showed in her voice.

"And what has your sister done now?" It was his turn to show impatience. This was not the first time that Naila had complained about her younger sister. In fact, the complaints had been coming more and more often as time went by.

"She embarrasses me constantly. She takes special pains to make me look ridiculous. It must stop. Even the Temple servants are laughing at me because of her."

"What would you have me do?"

"Day after tomorrow, I wish Kiera to be the Bride of Balim."

"It is not yet her time."

She walked around to the back of his chair and put her hands on his shoulders, gently massaging. "But you could order it if you wish. Please, Father, if you do this one thing for me, I'll not ask another favor."

This was not the first time she had made this very same promise, a promise that was always broken. "As I have said, it is not yet her time. Kiera has yet one more year. Choose another."

"I WANT KIERA." The venom fairly dripped from her words, so determined was she that she have her way.

"Naila, be reasonable. What will it gain?"

"It will put a stop to Leila's nonsense—that's what it will do." In her intensity, she gripped his shoulders enough to make him wince. Immediately sorry, she continued a gentle massage to remove the pain she so heedlessly had caused.

"If it means that much to you..." He paused only momentarily. "But, I'm warning you now, Naila, you cannot continue to disregard the rules of the Temple simply to satisfy your own personal desires. The people will not long stand for it. Nor will I." In actuality, he could refuse nothing to this his favorite daughter.

She now leaned over and kissed him gently on the cheek. "Thank you, Father. I promise it will not happen again."

As she closed the door behind her, she paused momentarily and a cruel little smile played across her lips. Her head held high with a regal and triumphant air, Naila, High Priestess of Balim and Initiate in the Ancient Mysteries, strode purposefully down the corridor to arrange her sister's "surprise party." She never tired of finding ways to make Leila uncomfortable but this was much better than anything she had done before, virtually the *coup de gras*. "This will teach that simpering sister of mine to cross me," she thought. "She will now know for certain who is High Priestess and WHO IS NOT."

A SAILING VACATION

"This is the happiest day of my life." Jennifer looked up with adoring eyes at David Craig, the football captain, who had just placed a diamond ring on her left hand. Life was beautiful; she and David had just been voted "Most Attractive Couple"; graduation was over; she had been accepted at Wellesly; and now had just become engaged.

The next three years were busy, busy, busy, what with school and working part time at Tomorrow's Woman as an assistant to the fashion editor. David was at Harvard and, though they didn't have a lot of time together, their love seemed to grow in leaps and bounds and they finally had set the date. It would be a December wedding with absolutely everyone in white; the only color would be the pink roses she would carry and her maid of honor and bridesmaids would have just the slightest touch of pink in their gowns.

The wedding was everything she had thought it would be and more. The church was a virtual winter fairyland and the reception was held in an ice palace decorated with pink rosebuds and green leaves. The orchestra was marvelous and they had danced the night away.

"DIVORCE GRANTED." The rap of the gavel and the judge's voice brought her back to the present and she looked up with a start. She looked at David. He looked as unhappy as she felt. For a very brief moment, she thought he was going to speak but he apparently changed his mind and turned to speak with his attorney instead. She stood silently for a few minutes more trying to decide whether or not to say anything to him when she suddenly realized that he was striding out of the courtroom.

As she left the courthouse, she hailed a cab. Tears welled up in her eyes. Nine years; she was married for nine years—and now it was over. Actually, it was over many years before, but she just did not want to admit her failure. And now that it was really, really over, she felt a little numb.

She changed her mind at the last moment and decided to walk back to her office. Her office—she, Jennifer Barron Craig, was considered a success. She WAS a success. At thirty-one, she was Fashion Editor of Today's world, a chic women's magazine with offices in downtown Manhattan. Not many women could point to such an accomplishment at so early an age. AND, though she was short by modern standards, she was considered quite comely. Her green eyes complimented quite nicely her blond hair and her healthy "girl-next-door" look. Yes, indeed, she WAS a success, wasn't she?

She once again slipped back into her reverie. She and David had been married almost two years and her joy was unsurpassed when it was learned she was pregnant. Her life was shattered when she miscarried at three months and the doctor told her that she would never be able to carry a child to full term. David could not adjust to this reality and now believed she did not want a child. This was far from the truth but she could not convince him and he would not hear of adoption. And the drinking began; David started sleeping in the guest room. While he continued to work, he now started staying out late and would arrive home with the smell of liquor on his breath and, sometimes, she would catch a slight odor of perfume when he would bend over her to kiss her on the forehead before going to his own bed.

And the abuse began; just a little shove at first, then a slap and once he actually gave her a "mouse." That was the end of their relationship for her. There was nothing for her to do but throw herself into her work. There were many, many nights of late, late hours, many passes and many promises but no fulfillment; and still more nights alone.

Then she met Tiffany Crist. Tiffany was a model and had lots of friends in the fashion world and Tiffany liked her. Well, "liked" probably was not exactly the right word, though "loved" was not exactly the right word either. She remembered now her shock and amazement the first time Tiffany kissed her. Her involuntary reaction was to pull away but Tiffany was both patient and demanding and finally Jen had come to truly care for this raven-haired beauty who was so powerful and so vulnerable at the same time.

Through Tiffany's influence, Jen's career skyrocketed and she became Assistant Fashion Editor, then Fashion Editor of Today's World, THE most prestigious magazine in THE most prestigious office—downtown Manhattan—in the States.

Her affair with Tiffany was relatively short-lived. While it was somewhat satisfying and a very necessary boost to her ego, there still was something missing. Besides, she still loved David and even though it was quite obvious even to her that her marriage was over, she continued to hope, in her overly optimistic and totally unrealistic fashion, that a miracle would happen and their lives would once again become that fairy tale romance that lived only in her dreams. More amazing was the fact that she and Tiffany remained the very closest of personal friends. Tiffany had many lovers, both male and female but, according to her, only one true friend and was willing to accept Jen on that basis once it was obvious that Jen did not have the same affinity for women as did she.

*   *   *

As she walked, her stride quickened; she felt a sudden elation and her spirits lifted. "I AM a success! I AM a success! I AM a success!" The thought stuck in her mind and the last nine years fell away as though they had never happened. She started to run and the sudden force of air blew her short hair up and back. She slowed her pace, did a little skip-step, totally unaware of her surroundings. This was the beginning of her life, NOT the end.

When she returned to the office, there was a message from Sim Barron, her favorite uncle. She called him back immediately. Although her elation remained, she could always use a friend. Sim and Helen were going on a cruise to Bermuda and invited her to come along. He said she might bring a guest. This was just what she needed—something to further lift her spirits. She was still talking to Sim when Tiffany walked in. "Sim, I think I'll take you up on that cruise and perhaps I'll bring Tiffany along. If she's willing?" She looked up expectantly.

Tiffany brightened and nodded her acceptance.

The next few days went by very quickly. She had to buy so many things and she packed and repacked several times before she was entirely satisfied with the wardrobe she was taking.

She and Tiffany took a Thursday evening flight to Miami and spent the next three days shopping and lying in the sun to get a tan. It would never do to go on a cruise without a tan.

*   *   *

November 30, …

Early Monday morning, they boarded The Seeker, fully prepared for a lot of sun and rest for the next two weeks. This was the first cruise for her, though Tiffany had been on several. She actually had met Tiffany through Alex Perrin, her uncle's employer and owner of The Seeker.

The Seeker! What a lovely name for a boat—yacht—whatever. She really did not know what to call it. Yesterday she had come down to the dock early in the morning, before Tiffany rose, to look around. She had been told that The Seeker was a yacht, was 110' long and could house as many as sixteen not including the crew. It was impressive but not THAT impressive. Of course, she had not actually been on a "yacht" before. In spite of her success, she did not really associate with the "yachting" crowd; she was more a country girl who just happened to live and work in the big city. She got back to the room before Tiffany woke and decided to say nothing of her little sortie. Her relationship with Tiffany was solid enough; however, she was loathe to let her know that naivete was her particular forte.

After getting settled in their cabin, they went out on deck to watch the other passengers come on board.

Alex was first to board and with him a tall, good-looking dark-haired man, whom he introduced as Reginald Masters. She had heard much about him, but then who hadn't? He was one of, if not THE, most eligible bachelor of the jet set. He was about fifteen years older than she and she wondered idly how he had managed to stay single so long.

She glanced over at Tiffany and saw the hungry look in her eyes. This Reginald Masters had better watch out or he might not be eligible much longer, at least not if Tiffany had anything to say about it and Tiffany pretty much got her own way.

Tiffany was an extremely beautiful woman and had been on the cover of Today's World many, many times. She was thirty-two, tall and slender, never had to diet, and had a complexion that was the envy of many women ten years and more her junior. At the age when most models are at the end of their careers, it seemed that Tiffany had just begun. She still was much in demand both in Europe and the United States and could pretty much write her own ticket.

Jennifer, on the other hand, was some three or four inches shorter than Tiffany and always had to fight her weight. Tiffany's eyes were riveted on Masters and Jen thought "It's about time Tiffany has someone positive in her love life. And who better than this handsome dark-haired giant who could, perhaps, give her some stability in her otherwise tempestuous love life." Jennifer mentally wished her friend the best of luck.

Next to board was an elderly gentleman who looked just like she remembered her grandfather to look. He was accompanied by a younger man who appeared quite concerned with the older man's comfort. Though she did not get to meet them, she later learned that this was Senator Wayne Danton from Texas and his aide, Donald Martin.

Last to arrive was her uncle Sim and his wife, Helen. Sim, too, had not had an easy life. He had been married before and had three children, now almost grown, but his first wife had caused him a lot of grief for a long, long time. Then he met Helen about seven years ago. They fell in love almost on sight and married within a week. From all appearances, they were now as ecstatically happy as when they first met.

It was close to midday when they got underway and she lay by herself on the deck enjoying the warmth of the noonday sun.

*   *   *

When she had walked into Jen's office last week, Tiffany was bored, bored, bored; and when Jen invited her on this cruise, she thought it was the answer to all her problems. AND, when she watched Reginald Masters board the yacht, it seemed like the answer to her "forever" prayer — just ONE time a beautiful relationship that would last forever. Only her "forever" never got started. She had not even SEEN this guy since then and they already had been on this stupid boat, on this STUPID ocean, on this STUPID cruise to NOWHERE for FIVE WHOLE DAYS that felt like as many weeks. She was tired of the sun, the sea, the wind, everything.

In a moment of desperation, she had even tried to renew her former love relationship with Jen but Jen said no and now she was reduced to using a vibrator, which was a far cry from real satisfaction. What she wanted right now was a man, ANY man. The big question was WHERE to find one out on this damned, god-forsaken ocean.

And, to add to her discomfort, the weather had been unseasonably hot. She had tried to sleep. God, she thought, will this heat never end? She glanced at her watch. Quarter past two. There was no relief even now.

She rose from her bed, glanced over to the other bed where Jen lay sleeping peacefully and gave a little sigh of desire and disappointment; it had been good while it lasted. She slipped into a filmy negligee and started for the door; maybe a walk on the deck would help. She saw a slight movement out of the corner of her eye and turned; it was only her image in the mirror. She stood for a moment admiring her form. She was truly beautiful. She knew it and did not hesitate to show it. Even in the semi-darkness, she could see the shape of her body through the negligee and ran her hands down her sides, from her breasts to her thighs and back again. She could feel the desire in her loins and continued caressing her body up and down while silently cursing out of her frustration. Why had she come on this trip anyway? She really cared for Jen but Jen had turned her away. Now, she was in the middle of the ocean, alone and unsatisfied.   The available men on this trip were either uninteresting or uninterested. Clearly frustrated, she gave forth a little moan, and with a final quick upward gesture with both hands, caressed her flat belly, and moving on up to her breasts, she pinched the nipples so hard she actually made them hurt.

She looked longingly at Jen one more time, then left the cabin. The night was still, not even a hint of a breeze. The velvet sky was studded with stars and, as the moon slipped playfully behind a wisp of cloud, she strolled aft.

*   *   *

December 6, ...

There was a light knock at the door. Masters opened one eye. Sun glinted on the metal edge of the porthole and he realized it was morning. He glanced automatically at his watch—11:52! He'd slept half the day away.

Muscles he didn't know he had screamed as he gingerly put one foot on the floor, then the other.

The knock sounded again.

"Who is it?"

"Charley, Mr. Reginald. I have some coffee for you."

"Come on in."

The door opened to reveal a black man of medium height carrying a tray containing a coffee carafe, cups, etc.

Masters could not remember a time when Charley had not been around. He was an almost constant companion to Alex Perrin. His great grandfather was a runaway slave who had been sheltered by the Perrin family. His grandmother managed the Perrin household, as did his mother Sarah until she married, at which time she left to make a home with her husband, a commercial fisherman. Charley's father was drowned when Charley was two years. Sarah had waited at the dock all night, even after she was told the news, believing that somehow her husband would return to her. When she was found the following morning, barely alive, she asked that the Perrin family be notified. Rockford Perrin paid for the best medical care to no avail, and granted Sarah's dying request that he rear her son as his own. When Alex was born some years later, Charley was devoted to him and, as Alex grew older, the two became fast friends. Although Charley had an excellent education, he chose a lesser role in order to remain close to his brother and friend. And, when he married, Charley brought his wife into the family as well.

Stepping inside the cabin, Charley placed the tray on a small table by the door and grinned widely, showing even, white teeth. "Missed you this morning, Mr. Reginald, and thought you might be needin' this. Everyone else has been up for hours. It sure is a beauty of a day." He did not even try to hide his glance toward the bed and, grinning once more, he backed out the door.

Masters sat on the edge of the bed a moment looking out the porthole. As Charley had said, it really was one "beauty of a day."

He gingerly got up and went to the tiny mirror above the portable wash basin. Good God, he thought, I look like I've been on a two-week drunk. He pulled down the basin and splashed water on his face, then quickly ran a shaver over his face and brushed his teeth. After combing his hair, he appraised himself once again in the mirror.

For all his forty-seven years, Reginald Masters was still quite handsome. He had soft, dark brown hair, a little unruly but which only added to his boyish good looks and complimented a close-cut beard and mustache. A touch of gray simply enhanced the enigma surrounding his personna. His clear blue eyes rivaled tempered steel when flashing angrily, yet sparkled mischievously with his ready smile. Six foot four in his stocking feet, he had the well-muscled physique of a professional athlete.

*   *   *

He walked over the to the coffee tray; poured himself a cup of coffee; and pulled the only chair in the room a little closer to the bed. Sliding down into it, he stretched out his legs to rest his feet on the edge of the bed. As he sipped his coffee, he thought about last night.

He had decided to take a turn around the deck before he called it a night and now stood alone leaning against the stern railing looking out over the black water. There were a few high clouds playing tag with a half-full moon and the stars winked in and out like sun-tipped ripples on a mountain lake in winter.

It was the end of the fifth day since they had left San Juan on the "annual" cruise hosted by Alex Perrin, his longtime friend, and thus far the trip had been utterly boring—and there were nine more days of this sameness to look forward to. The only change in routing this year was their destination: Bermuda.

Just this once, he thought prophetically, it would be a welcome relief if something different or out of the ordinary would happen. Hearing a sound behind him, he turned to see a shadowy figure coming toward him. Just then, the moon re-emerged in its full glory from behind a cloud and he saw Tiffany Crist. "And it just did," he said aloud.

"What did?" She asked. As she walked unabashedly toward him, he could see her slender body silhouetted in the moonlight. She was barefoot and, at that, she was almost as tall as he. She wore the sheerest and shortest of negligees and there was absolutely nothing left to the imagination.

Frank admiration showed in his face as he looked at her breasts which, though small, were full and firm. He could see the nipples proudly pushing outward against the flimsy material. Her thick, dark hair reached just short of her waist and contrasted strikingly with her "peaches and cream" complexion. In the moonlight, her long shapely legs were exquisitely carved ivory.

"An angel has come to rescue me from tedium."

She moved closer. He felt a stirring in his loins as she coyly ran her fingers up his arm. "Well?" She asked.

"Well, what?"

Her body was now touching his. The scent of her perfume wafted upward like a heady cloud, sharpening his senses. She pressed still closer and he felt the hot fire of desire. She looked directly into his eyes. "Do I pass your inspection?" Her husky voice made the question an open invitation.

*   *   *

His thoughts winged back to the present and he glanced over at the bed. Tiffany was still asleep. Angel, indeed! It was difficult, even now, to believe that this sleeping beauty was last night's barracuda.

They had slowly walked to his stateroom, his appetite whetted by anticipation.

He opened his stateroom door and she walked through with a regal air. She was barely inside when she shrugged her shoulders slightly and the negligee fell to the floor. He reached for the switch to turn out the light but she put her hand on his arm.

"No. I want to see you."

With one swift motion he stepped out of his trunks and sneakers and pulled her down onto the bed. She fairly melted into his arms. THEN, with a strength her looks denied, she put her legs around his thighs and rolled over so that she was on top. He was taken aback by this but intrigued also. She put her mouth on his in a sweet "hello" kiss, then ran the tip of her tongue over his lips as though "exploring the territory" and all the while her hands were caressing his upper torso and she was gently rocking back and forth massaging his cock with her pussy. He could see this was going to be one delightful experience and surrendered himself to her manipulations.

Suddenly, and ferociously, she bit his lower lip until he could taste the blood, then thrust her hardened tongue deep into his mouth just like a tiny penis, at the same time digging her fingernails into his buttocks. He gave a start and a muffled cry of surprise and she ceased her actions as quickly as they had begun and emitted a low humming sound and resumed her rocking motion and her exploration kiss.

He relaxed and, encouraged by this, she moved her hands to the base of his cock and gently massaged it. He still was wary but the manipulation of her fingers brought forth a delightful sensation and a kind of hunger he had never before felt so he relaxed further. She raised herself slightly and, placing her pussy on the tip of his cock, pushed downward.

"What a beautiful cock you have." It was more a low, guttural moan than a statement and, if it were possible, his desire became even stronger. She still had her hands on his cock and now he felt he could no longer contain his passion, so he gave in to his desire which seemed to burst forth. But, what was this? He had reached a climax surely. He knew it. But, it did not stop. Amazement turned to pleasure, and pleasure to the point of pain. Tiffany moved her hands and his release was momentous. How did she do that?

A strange, curious thought—had she climaxed as well? His climax was so large he really couldn't be sure. If not, then he must take care of her but, really, he was ready to call it quits. The sensation was tremendous but he felt drained and just wanted to sleep. That was not to be. He may not be able to take care of her, but she certainly was going to take care of him. She had slid down between his legs and now put that sweet, angelic, demonic mouth over the tip of his cock and was running her tongue up and down, all around and even tried to put it inside. She was again using her fingers as well on his balls and at the base of his cock. He did not think it possible but he was again swelling with desire.

Time and again, she brought forth his desire, a desire he seemingly could not control—did not have the energy to control—did not believe was possible but it was actually happening to him. AND, as far as he could tell, she climaxed at least every time he did. There was no stopping her—or himself, it seemed.

He had known aggressive women before but this one put them all to shame. She was sensual in every way; however, he was totally unprepared for her demands and was grateful when she finally had fallen asleep. He had always thought himself quite a stud and, as yet, had no complaints in the sex department. Even now, he was loathe to admit being bested by a woman and would most certainly deny it if asked, but this woman was just a little too much for him. Did he say a LITTLE too much? She was a LOT too much for him. It had been quite an experience; one he would not soon forget, but one he also was not eager to repeat.

Never one for too much introspection, Masters tried to shake off his feeling of inadequacy. Now he was forced to admit to himself that maybe, just maybe, he should re-evaluate his life style. Maybe it was just about time he started acting his age.

VACATION TURNED NIGHTMARE

He had just reached for the coffee pot to pour himself another cup when there was a sudden lurch. The coffee tray slid off onto the floor with a clatter and the tinkle of breaking glass. Still holding the carafe and his cup, he managed to get to his feet. Another lurch! Setting down the carafe and cup, he grabbed his trunks while slipping his feet into his sneakers. He pulled on his trunks as he headed for the door.

Tiffany stirred sleepily. "What's going on?"

Without pausing, he called back over his shoulder, "I'm going to find out. You'd better stay here." She started to speak again but just then there was another shock. This time Masters was completely off balance and went down on one knee. Recovering quickly, however, he headed for the deck. It was difficult keeping his balance as he made his way up the ladder. He stopped short.

THEY HAD SAILED INTO HELL!

*　　*　　*

Captain Davis had just finished checking his instruments and leaned back in his chair. What a sorry pass this was. He should be grateful for this one last chance. Had Alex Perrin not been willing to risk hiring a "drunk," his career would have been over long ago.

His mind still could not fully accept what had happened that night two years ago. Because of his drinking, his wife Martha would be a cripple the rest of her life. Not that she blamed him; far from it. She was so damned understanding. Why couldn't it have been he instead of her? They had been driving up the coast on a holiday weekend. Even now, the thought of the truck careening toward them, jack-knifing when the driver tried to avoid the collision, yet sliding into the camper on Martha's side, still created a hard knot in the pit of his stomach. Involuntarily, he put his hands over his ears to shut out Martha's screams and unwanted tears squeezed through tightly closed eyelids.

He was shaken from his reverie when he felt the boat lurch. How long had he been sitting here day-dreaming? A quick glance at his watch told him it had been no more than ten minutes yet, seemingly, they had drifted into a fierce storm. He checked his instruments—they were gyrating wildly. His heart skipped a beat—he remembered his conversation with Alex Perrin when he was hired on. When told they would be sailing from Miami to Bermuda via Puerto Rico, he had glibly said "You want to take on the Devil's Triangle? I'm your man. I've seen his worst; he's not so tough." Now the very thought struck a note of fear in his heart. Why had he taunted Satan?

He reached for the radio and started his May Day broadcast.

* * *

Slipping and sliding, Masters made his way onto the deck. The sky was black as night and winds were tearing at the tiny craft, batting it first one way and then the other. Everything not tied down went overboard; waves washed the deck and salt spray stung his uncovered torso. He fought his way along the railing, finding such handholds as he could and worked his way around the hatch and up the ladder to the bridgehouse. The wind tore the door from his grasp as he turned the knob and, with a rush, carried him inside. Barely maintaining his balance and with great physical effort, he managed to close the door behind him. His skin was red from the lashing of the wind and the sea, and he was almost blinded from the salty spray. Taking great gulps of air, he leaned against the door of the bridgehouse until his heart stopped its wild pacing, and he was able to take stock of himself and the room.

Captain Davis was seated at the radio, leaning slightly forward, the mike in his hand. "FN3892 calling Coast Guard! FN3892 calling Coast Guard! May Day! May Day! Our approximate position is Longitude 66 degrees West, Latitude 26 degrees North. We are encountering northeasterly winds at 100 to 120 miles per hour. FN3892 calling Coast Guard! FN3892 calling…" There was a sputtering sound, some sparks, and the radio went dead.

Davis dropped the mike resignedly. "Well, that's that."

"Davis, what happened?"

"It's one of those freak storms that occur in this area." Davis had to yell to make himself heard above the roar of the wind. "One minute the sky is clear, the next it's pitch black with gale winds. It lasts anywhere from thirty minutes to three hours. I've never been in one myself, but I know a couple guys who have. From what they tell me, probably the worst that will happen is that we'll be blown off course."

"Well, Davis," Masters said, "you seem to have everything under control here. I'd better get below and see how the others are faring.

He paused momentarily, thinking about the wind outside, then reached for the door. He braced himself for the blast of air as he turned the knob and was surprised that it was not forthcoming. He went out, closing the door behind him. He went down the ladder and was making his way around the hatch when he felt the deck shift beneath his feet. He lost his footing and caught the door frame just in time to keep from falling. Suddenly, the whole sky was illuminated by a bright and burning light. As suddenly as it had come, it was gone. But that instant was enough. The boat was spinning at an every-increasing speed. NO! That was not quite right … it was the world that was spinning … or was it he? It was all quite confusing. He fought both vertigo and nausea, and as he entered into the dark, deep well of unconsciousness, he realized they had NOT sailed into Hell. Impossible though it may be, THEY WERE SAILING RIGHT OFF THE EDGE OF THE WORLD!

PHILADELPHIA FREEDOM NEWS
Philadelphia, PA December 6, …
SOS SIGNAL FROM PERRIN YACHT
Coast Guard and Navy Combine for Search

API, Miami, FL

At approximately 12:05 EST today, a May Day was received by the Coast Guard from The Seeker, a 110' yacht belonging to millionaire Alex Perrin, placing the craft about midway between Puerto Rico and Bermuda.

Apparently caught in a freak storm, The Seeker reported encountering 100-120 mph winds before radio control was lost.

The Coast Guard, joined by the Navy, immediately launched a massive air and sea search of the area. Several civilian pilots have also joined in the search.

For the past several years, Perrin, joined by several friends, has cruised the Bahamas and the Gulf of Mexico. This year the cruise destination was to be Bermuda.

* * *

Alex Perrin, son of Rockford Perrin, newspaper publisher, is noted for his work with boys' clubs and the establishment of free youth centers in several eastern cities, including Chicago and Boston. He has extensive interests in oil and shipping, which include Lasko Oil Company, Alpine Oil Refinery and Marietta S.S. Lines.

Senator and Playboy Aboard

Wayne Danton (D.TX), also a passenger aboard the Perrin yacht, entered politics at the age of 28. In his fifth term as a U. S. Senator, Danton is currently Chairman of the Senate Banking & Currency Subcommittee.

Reginald C. Masters, III, is the son of steel magnate, R. C. Masters, Jr. His many accomplishments include setting a new speed record at Daytona, and he is currently financing a new turbine engine which is to be tried this coming year at Indianapolis. Masters is the owner of a professional hockey team, The Northern Lights, and in 1995 he set up a foundation for research on new drugs to aid in controlling the AIDS virus.

Other passengers aboard The Seeker include J. Simpson Barron, Chief Executive Officer of Lasko Oil Company, and his wife, Helen; Jennifer Barron Craig, Fashion Editor of Today's World; Donald Martin, Aide to Senator Danton; and Tiffany Crist, model and cover girl.

The crew included John N. Davis, Captain; Charles Washington, personal valet to Alex Perrin; Clifford Evans, Engineer; William Paulson; Robert Larson; Jack Stone; Fred Graham; and Skip Norton.

A NEW WORLD

Masters awakened to an easy, rolling motion. Everything was quiet; the only sound he heard was the waves gently washing against the side of the boat.

What a nightmare! It was enough to make one stay awake forever.

He took a deep breath and became acutely aware of a pain in his chest. My God, it was real! Recall came quickly now—the storm; the SOS. He shuddered as he remembered that awful black gulf—falling, falling into absolute nothingness—the breath literally born from his lungs. Involuntarily, he gasped for breath and once again felt the searing pain in his lungs.

He looked about and discovered he was at the bottom of the stern ladder. He must have fallen when he blacked out. He quickly checked to see that no bones were broken and then slowly rose to his feet. It was still difficult to breathe, but he thought he could manage. Force of habit caused him to glance at his watch—1:15. He looked away, then quickly back again—1:15? He must have been out for an hour or more. What about the others? He had been on his way to check on them when he had lost consciousness.

As he started down the passageway, the door to Perrin's stateroom opened and Perrin stepped out. "Masters?"

"Alex, are you all right?"

"I seem to be. We had just come down to freshen up before lunch and that's the last I remember. Do you know what happened?"

Masters quickly recounted what had happened up to the time he passed out. "I was just on my way down to see if everyone is okay, but two of us can do it much faster. Even if Davis' message got through and the Coast Guard is on its way, we'll have to manage for ourselves until it gets here."

Perrin nodded, opened one of the stateroom doors and stepped inside.

Masters remembered Tiffany and turned to his own stateroom, just opposite the one Perrin had entered. She was still on the bed … white as the sheet that partially covered her. He leaned over to listen for a heartbeat and, at the same time, caught up her left wrist to feel for her pulse. None. He reached up to touch her carotid artery. The pulse was there but it was slight.

He sprang to the small liquor cabinet in the corner of the room, hoping fervently that at least one of the bottles was unbroken. Luck was with him and he grabbed a bottle of Napoleon brandy. Tearing out the cork, he hurried back to the bed. He squeezed the sides of her mouth together until her lips parted slightly, and let a little brandy trickle into her mouth. She choked as the fiery liquid went down, gasped for air, and sat up. She opened her eyes and stared blankly as she struggled to catch her breath. "What's going on?" she demanded.

"It's obvious you're okay." he responded sarcastically. "Haven't time to explain right now." Taking the bottle, he bolted out the door.

Perrin was not in sight, so he opened the door to the adjoining stateroom which was occupied by Senator Danton and his aide.

Senator Danton was a tired, old man. He had fought many battles in Congress—had won some; had lost some. Now, he was fighting his last battle—a battle he could not win, but he refused to surrender; though only sixty-eight, the Senator was dying of cancer.

The Senator was in a semi-upright position with his assistant hovering over him. Danton seemed to be having a little trouble breathing, but Masters knew that would soon pass. Young Martin looked okay, his only concern apparently the Senator. Masters decided he was not needed here.

As he turned away from the Senator's door, he bumped into Perrin, who had just come out of the stateroom directly opposite. "The Barrons and Ms. Craig are fine, but I can't find Ms. Crist. Did you see her?"

"Tiffany's fine and Martin is taking care of the Senator. They both looked okay to me. That takes care of everyone but the crew."

They turned in the direction of the crew's quarters in time to see Charley coming up the passageway. "Except for a few cuts and bruises, they're just fine, Mr. Reginald," he said.

"Thanks, Charley," Perrin said. "Well, Reg, are you about ready to see how much damage the storm did?"

Perrin walked up the passageway toward the stern ladder and started up, Masters and Charley following close behind. He started out on deck, then stopped short, causing Masters to bump into him with Charley following suit.

"What the…?" Masters exclaimed.

But Perrin showed no immediate inclination to move further. Masters pushed by him and on up the ladder out onto the deck. Then he saw what was wrong. He saw it, but he didn't believe it. The sun was all wrong. The sky was clear and blue, but the sun, instead of being bright white as it should have been at this time of day, was red-gold and he could look directly at it without squinting. And that wasn't the only thing. There was a definite chill, although there was no breeze and it was only about 2:00 p.m. He shivered—not entirely from the coolness of the air. Where were they? This didn't look like the North Atlantic. But then, where? That sun really bothered him.

Now that he was on deck, Masters noticed yet another change. "Alex, come on up here. This is absolutely incredible. Either my nose is deceiving me, or the salt smell is gone—and look at the water." It was no longer green. It was blue—definitely blue—one of the clearest, deepest blues he had ever seen, almost purple.

Perrin and Charley came out of the doorway and Perrin sniffed the air, a puzzled frown on his face, then "Charley, get me a bucket—on the double!" He was leaning over the side, "And some rope," he yelled after the disappearing black man.

Charley returned quickly with the bucket, several lengths of rope and a tin cup—at times he was positively uncanny.

Masters started to take the bucket, realized he still had the bottle of brandy in his hand, took a long pull, and offered it to Perrin. Perrin shook his head and Masters gave it to Charley to put away. He and Perrin then proceeded to tie a length of rope, as best they could, to the thin bail of the bucket and tossed it over the side.

They were just pulling up the bucket filled with water when Masters caught a flicker of light out of the corner of his eye. He looked up quickly. Nothing! It had appeared to be the glint of sun on metal, but now it was gone.

Shaking his head as though to clear it of cobwebs, he now dipped the cup into the water and raised it to his lips. "Just as I suspected," he said. "This water is fresh."

Another pinprick of light on the water caught his attention. This time it did not disappear. "Do you see that, Alex? I think we're going to find out what's up pretty soon because someONE or someTHING is coming out to pay us a call."

While waiting for the object to get close enough to identify, Masters and Perrin decided to look around and see if any major damage was done. Two crewmen had come up on deck and were going about their duties and effecting minor repairs. For all its fury, the storm had unexpectedly caused relatively little damage.

Jennifer felt the soft rocking motion of the boat. Her eyes still closed, she started to stretch but something was blocking her way. Recall came quickly as she opened her eyes and realized she was on the floor of the cabin she shared with Tiffany.

She had come down looking for Tiffany and to get her suntan lotion before going out on deck for some more sun when the boat gave a sudden lurch. She lost her balance and put out her arm to catch herself—that was all she could remember.

Now, the door opened behind her and she raised herself up on one elbow and turned to see if it might be Tiffany. She had not seen her since last night in a vague remembrance of a soft touch and Tiffany had not slept in her bed. At least she was gone when Jen had awakened at about 5:00 a.m.

"Jen, are you all right?" It was Alex. When she assured him she was, he asked "Have you seen Tiffany? Reg and I are checking to see that everyone is okay."

"No, I haven't. Do you know what happened?"

"Not yet. We're going to check on that now and will let you know as soon as we know."

He left then and she raised herself up to a sitting position and looked around. The room was a mess—and so was she. The bottle she had been holding was broken and suntan lotion was everywhere. She cleaned it up and changed her clothes and went up on deck to see if she could learn anything new.

As she arrived topside, she was taken aback momentarily at the change she saw and the consternation on the faces of Perrin and Masters. However, not one to be daunted by the new and unexplained, she was determined to make the best of the situation. She looked younger than her thirty-one years, was of medium height and had the kind of figure that needs no artificial aids. Her honey-colored hair was worn in a page-boy and her green eyes sparkled with excitement and anticipation as she did a pirouette and spread her golden arms to embrace the sky. "Isn't it marvelous? I feel as though I could just fly away."

She was wearing a pair of white shorts and a green and white striped tank top that left little to the imagination, and both men looked at her with a mixture of admiration and amazement. Here was a young woman, thought Masters, a child actually, who had apparently discarded all fear of the unknown in the romance of the situation.

"Oh," squealed Jen. "Look!" Both men turned to follow her pointing finger. The object was now about one and one-half miles away and, at first glance, it appeared to be a huge dome with a small extension on top. It came to within about thirty feet off the port stern, then proceeded to describe a complete circle around the yacht, and stopped.

It was made of some sort of metal that looked almost like copper, but had a satin-like finish rather than a polished surface. Masters could now see that there was a flange encircling the craft at the water line, apparently some type of stabilizer to keep it from capsizing. He estimated the flange to be approximately twenty feet in width and the craft itself to be a good forty to fifty feet high. The smaller section on top was obviously some kind of cockpit or bridge and contained the only windows. He could see no doors at all.

On a section facing the yacht, about fifteen feet above the flange, was an insignia. As nearly as he could tell, there were three intertwining rings, one each in red, blue, and green. It was difficult to be really sure because they were in continuous motion, almost like marquee lights, marching forever in a preordained pattern.

Except for Sim and Helen Barron coming out on deck to see what was going on, the scene remained unchanged for what seemed like forever.

*   *   *

Nikto stood just inside the entrance to the Great Hall awaiting yet another sacrifice to Balim; another young maiden scheduled to meet her bridegroom. Off to one side, he saw the curtains sway gently and tried to see the cause. There was someone there but he could not quite make out who it was; that it was a woman in service to the Temple he knew by her clothing and its color - pale blue.

At the moment of possible discovery, he was distracted by the chimes; the procession had begun. He turned his attention to the proceedings and awaited the second sounding of the chimes and the tinkle of silver upon silver that heralded the arrival of Naila—his beautiful Naila. Once, long ago, he had dared to ask her father D'Ar, High Priest of Balim, for her hand in Alliance and, amazingly, D'Ar consented; such Alliance would give Nikto much power and prestige and, apparently, D'Ar seemed to see some value in it for himself as well.

Things such as these take much time, however, and Nikto, for all his training in the ways of the Temple, was getting

23

impatient. He wanted his future assured now, before D'Ar returned to Balim. After all, D'Ar, having passed beyond his sixteenth dakar, was no longer considered in his prime and it already had been rumored that he planned to name Naila his successor in the near future. In anticipation of this event, D'Ar had already bestowed upon her the title of High Priestess of Balim. Once named his successor, Naila would have no need for Alliance and this did not suit Nikto. His whole service to the Temple was predicated on and pointed toward this Alliance and what he could gain from it.

Not that Naila was some dowdy old maid who had lived beyond her Alliance years, although she HAD passed four dakars some time ago (most maidens formed Alliance before reaching the end of four dakars). Indeed, her beauty was incomparable; she was almost as tall as he and certainly had the grace and bearing of a goddess. But he did not love Naila, for she was as hard as she was beautiful; more like an alabaster statue than a woman. However, one must take risks to gain the coveted prize and Nikto was ready to make the supreme sacrifice to gain the power which he desired so greatly.

He now watched Naila as she proceeded slowly to the altar. Was that a gleam of satisfaction he caught in her eye as she glanced around the hall? The movement of a curtain had halted her survey and he saw a tiny cruel smile curve her otherwise perfect lips. He turned in that direction and again saw that flash of blue. Who could it be? Her face still was hidden from him but Naila knew full well who it was, of that he was certain.

He continued to watch until D'Ar, who was immediately behind Naila, had mounted the steps to the altar, then he turned away. Power was that for which he thirsted, not blood. Nor did he see the necessity of blood sacrifice. This would all change when he… He shook his head to clear away the last tentacles of his dream future; now was not the time. Duty called and there was much to be done; he must see if Balim had afforded D'Ar yet more victims to slake his thirsty blade.

He strode away from the hall and down a long corridor leading to the dock where his craft and crew were waiting. As he gave the order to proceed, he thought about this somewhat onerous task—searching the Lake of Kaos after each Day of Sacrifice to see if new, unwary travelers had been sucked down into the Eye of Balim. This gave him little pleasure, for the survival of these strangers, these otherworlders, was tenuous at best. If D'Ar found them unsuitable for the altar, they joined the many minions of Balim who toiled endlessly in the pits where Balim reigned in a more physical sense and often fell victim to his wrath there, where a misstep could result in the loss of limb or sight and, ultimately, loss of life. No imperfections were allowed in Balim's realm, whether above or below; such was the decree of this one-eyed god who knew neither love nor mercy for his worshipers.

The sun was high when a touch of white showed on the horizon. Nikto was disappointed at the first "hallo." His hopes of a fruitless trip once more dashed, he set his course with a grim determination. Whether or not he ever had Naila, or the power she might bring, it was now time to take a stand. For long he had been aware of unrest and dissatisfaction in Encandor and even in the Temple itself. He could close his eyes to the slaughter no longer. And now, he must present still more victims for Balim's insatiable appetite? NOT IF HE COULD HELP IT. NO power was worth this contrived mockery of a religion OR the bondage into which he had so willingly sold himself.

A mixture of relief and elation flooded through his senses. The decision had been made; he would end his self-enslavement and break the chains of greed that had held him so long. This new freedom of mind brought with it a feeling much like that which came from drinking timson, a light but potent spirit which released the senses to full enjoyment.

By this time, they had come within hailing distance of a strange small craft. Unlike the boats of iron he was accustomed to, this one was much smaller, clearly made of wood and had cloth hangings strung from what appeared to be tall poles rising from its middle. There was another long pole which seemed to reach almost from the middle to one end of the boat and apparently was the anchor for the cloth hangings.

With a quick, single motion, he ordered a full stop, the better to survey this otherworld vessel and, hopefully, to learn the complement before boarding. He wanted no mishaps, no injuries. Seeing only a few persons on deck, he gave the order to circle the craft and prepare for boarding.

The pilot made a full circle of the craft, started to raise the craft out of the water and move toward the yacht but, unused to such a small craft, overshot the edge of the strange boat and, in trying to correct his error, broke off a piece of the wooden railing. There was no other mishap, however, and Nikto gave the order to board these new otherworlders.

*   *   *

Nerves were becoming frayed and anticipation was turning to frustration when, finally, the strange craft, to their amazement, started to rise out of the water. There was no evidence of rotors or jets and yet it was going straight up. It continued to rise until the flange was even with the deck of the yacht. Watching closely, Masters now realized that the craft was a sphere rather than just a dome as he had first thought.

It started to move toward them. The small group on deck backed away slowly, but was soon stopped by the starboard railing. There was a crackling sound as the flange cut through a portion of the port railing. Splinters flew in all directions as one section broke completely off and was pushed before the flange for about ten feet. Then the craft stopped.

Masters heard a small cry behind him and turned just in time to see Helen Barron swoon in her husband's arms. Masters had not known the Barrons for long, and knew only that Sim Barron worked for one of Alex Perrin's companies and that Helen was his second wife.

Fascination held the tiny group rooted to the deck as, directly below the insignia, a vertical slit appeared in the sphere and started to widen slowly. On each side of the opening a section of the sphere was sliding back into the craft and, when the motion finally stopped, the opening was about ten feet wide at the bottom, some two feet narrower at the top, and the overall height was about ten feet.

Masters could see a faint light which appeared to be some distance back inside the opening, and he moved a short distance forward across the deck toward the strange craft in order to get a better look inside. He stopped just short of the flange and tried to peer into the craft. He had little time, however, for just moments later three men appeared in the doorway, the one in the center slightly ahead of the other two. Masters breathed a sigh of relief—at least they appeared to be human. The three men were somewhat taller than average and quite muscular. Decidedly, Masters would not like to test their skill in hand-to-hand combat.

The three were dressed alike in costumes of a shiny metallic-like cloth, which molded to their bodies like a second skin. Each wore a belt that was about three inches wide and contained several squares of a hard, black substance. These squares were about an inch thick and had a button or stud near the bottom. The fitted pants ended in heavy boots which were covered with the same material and had soles about an inch thick with slightly higher heels. The shirt had a high, round neckline with no collar, and sleeves that ended at the wrist.

At the left shoulder on the front of the shirt was the insignia which appeared on the craft and, below that was yet another insignia: a dark blue ring with a silver triangle through it, so that only the tips of the triangle were outside the ring.

Each man wore a silver-colored helmet with the ship insignia in front, and which had slight protrusions over the ears. On each of these protrusions was a small button from which extended a tiny antenna.

Masters could see nothing that looked like any type of weapon, and the only difference in the uniforms of the three was the color—all three were blue; however, while two were extremely pale, the third was a royal blue, and it was this third man who now spoke.

"In the name of D'Ar, I welcome you to Encandor. I am Nikto." He paused momentarily, motioned the two men to one side, then turned toward the doorway and issued a command in a strange language. Immediately, about a dozen men in pale blue uniforms moved out onto the deck of the yacht. Masters noted that these men certainly had weapons, even if the first three did not.

These weapons were attached to the belt in some manner that was not readily visible from where Masters was standing. The handle was thick and had a grip not unlike the handle of an old-fashioned home-movie camera. On the thumb side of the handle were three buttons which could be depressed into the handle. The end of the barrel was flared to about three inches in diameter, making it look like a tiny megaphone.

It was an interesting firearm and one which Masters certainly would like to see at close range; provided, of course, it was not pointed in his direction. If it fired missiles of some sort, it could make a very nasty hole.

The men, who were either soldiers or police of some sort, spread out over the deck, some standing at the open doorways, others going down the various ladders to the passengers' and crews' quarters, and one had been dispatched to check the wheelhouse. They appeared to be quite adept at this procedure, and Masters wondered if there was a possibility this predicament had happened to others previously. He was still puzzled as to how he and the others had gotten here in the first place, and where they were now that they were here. The word "Encandor" was totally alien to him and did not convey too much information. And, then, there was the matter of the language. He was sure that in his extensive travels he had never heard this particular language.   Besides, at least one of the men spoke English.

He was startled from his speculation when one of the soldiers returned to the deck from the passengers' quarters and spoke briefly in the strange language.   Nikto made a comment and pointed to the doorway of the alien craft.   The soldier went inside only to appear scant moments later pushing a chair—a chair that was floating in mid-air!   He pushed it over to the ladder and started down.

From what he had seen thus far, it was obvious to Masters that here was a race far advanced over his own—at least advanced enough technologically to have discovered the principle of anti-gravity.   His immediate concern, however, was the reason for the chair.   He wondered what might have occurred to require such a device.

The answer was not long in coming.   Two of the soldiers had just started up the stern ladder with Tiffany.   Each one had hold of one arm and were propelling her slightly ahead of them.   She was resisting slightly.   No longer in the clothing from the night before, she now wore a tiny sunsuit of a soft, pink material and high-heeled platform shoes—definitely not the proper dress for this place and time and he saw her shiver as she was pushed out into the cool air.   Directly behind this trio was Donald Martin and, behind him, two more soldiers.   Then came the soldier pushing the chair and in it, slumped over, was Senator Danton. It was apparent from his face that he was in considerable pain. The breathing problem should have passed long before now, and Masters was deeply concerned for this stately old man with his unruly shock of white hair.

By the time this little procession had come to a halt, the soldiers who had gone to the crews' quarters were returning to the deck.   There were many questions and much muttering as the soldiers gathered the group together, with the Senator slightly apart. Martin was allowed to stay by his side.

Masters felt a hand on his arm.   "I don't see Davis anywhere." It was Perrin. "I wonder where he could be." The two of them very quickly checked with the crew members, but none had seen him for several hours.

Charley edged in to get close to Masters. "Mr. Reginald, after I checked on the crew earlier, I went up to see about Captain Davis. He wasn't there. I looked everywhere I could think of, but I couldn't find him. I haven't told Mr. Alex because I didn't want to get the captain in trouble, but he sometimes takes a bottle of whisky and goes off by himself for a few hours. Nobody is sure just where, but I reckon that's where he is now.

Masters relayed the message to Perrin, and they decided it was better not to mention at this point that one of the crew was missing. As for Davis, if the soldiers did not find him, there was plenty of food on board the yacht and if they were in trouble, as they might well be, it would be good to have someone who was free to move around—assuming, of course, that he could move around undetected in this strange world.

Nikto cleared his throat. "You will be taken to Encandor aboard our ship and your own vessel will be towed into port. Please go as you are directed."

Nikto stationed one of the soldiers at the door of the craft with a slate on which he made notes, presumably to identify each of the group as they entered the craft.

The Senator and Martin were the first to be escorted aboard by three soldiers, one on either side and one pushing the chair in which the Senator sat; then the women, accompanied by Sim Barron because Helen would not let go of his arm. Following them were Charley and the crew, leaving Masters and Perrin to bring up the rear.

Upon entering the craft, Masters noted that, although the interior had appeared quite dark from outside, he was able to see clearly in his immediate area. Ahead, however, it was still very dim—so dim, in fact, that he could barely make out the forms of those in front of him. He turned to look back and noted that the door was already closed. He looked up and to the sides but could find no source of the light, yet there seemed to always be light enough for him to walk comfortably, just not enough for him to see very far in any direction.

They were conducted through a corridor which led to the center of the ship and a circular dais, upon which Masters observed two shafts, each approximately six feet in diameter. These shafts contained what appeared to be a blue, translucent liquid or semi-liquid substance which was flowing—swirling, actually—constantly in a vertical direction; the one on his right was moving in an upward direction and the one on his left downward. The shafts passed through both ceiling and floor.

Masters and Perrin stopped before the dais and soon were joined by Nikto. "This is our Access Shaft. I believe you call it an elevator or lift. To use it, one merely steps in and is carried up or down one level at a time." He indicated that they should enter the shaft.

"Just a minute," said Masters. "We'd like to know what this is all about and you seem to know, so how about it?"

"All in good time. But for the moment, please accompany me. I will show you to the quarters you will occupy while you are on board." He gestured again and the three of them entered the upward-moving shaft together.

Masters' first inclination was to hold his breath. It was like walking into a steady stream of light-weight oil. He had a slight sensation of rising that stopped so quickly he was not really sure he had felt it all. However, he felt Nikto touch his arm and the three men moved forward out of the shaft onto a dais identical to the one they had just quitted, though this one was better lit. Had it not been for the different lighting and the fact that he saw some of the others as he stepped out of the shaft, he would not have believed they had changed levels at all; perhaps it was merely an illusion and they still were where they started.

As he stepped from the shaft, he impulsively brushed at his arms and chest; however, felt nothing but hair and skin. He shrugged his shoulders and stepped from the dais into a circular hallway which had dissecting corridors at four equi-distant points, dividing the sphere into four separate sections, each section containing two doors. It was to one of these doors that Nikto now directed them. "These are your quarters." With this he turned and stepped back onto the dais. As he entered the upward Access Shaft, it began to shimmer, continuing for a few seconds, then faded.

Masters and Perrin had just finished a cursory inspection of the room, which disclosed it to be amazingly well-equipped to serve their immediate needs, but certainly not meant for a long pleasure cruise, when a knock sounded at the door. Masters opened it to find a soldier with a package. "I have clothing for you, sirs, and I am to take you to the dining hall when you are ready."

The mention of dining made Masters check the time: 5:30! He had lost all track of time in the excitement and now he realized he was quite hungry. "Thank you," he murmured, anxious to get on with it.

As he closed the door, Masters saw the soldier turn his back to the wall and assume an alert position. It may mean nothing at all—perhaps habit—but the thought once again came to mind that they might be prisoners. He was not at all sure he liked this development. However, as there was not much he could do about it at the moment, he decided he might as well make the best of it.

He and Perrin quickly showered and shaved, then turned their attention to the package of clothing left by the soldier. It contained two uniforms, not unlike those worn by the men they had seen thus far, except that they were of a pale green color and had a dark green stripe, about two inches wide, which ran diagonally across the breast from the right shoulder to the waist. The circle and triangle decorated the left shoulder and the belt was a plain black band.

Now that he had it on, Masters could marvel at this costume. It was a perfect fit and the material had a peculiar quality which caused it to hug the body while it did not bind in any way and, although the cloth was extremely lightweight, it had a heat-conducting property, because he was now quite comfortable, where before he had been slightly chilled.

All their preparations completed, the two men wandered out into the corridor. There, with the exception of Sim Barron, were all the men from The Seeker, some walking about and others whispering in small groups. Masters noted that all were dressed in the same manner as he and Perrin. The Senator was there also with Martin hovering over him.

He started to walk toward the Senator when he felt a hand on his arm. "Where are the women?" Perrin was hesitant in his speech, which was quite unlike him. He was usually very forceful. It was now apparent to Masters just how much this "adventure" had affected Alex, though by outward appearances he was holding up very well.

"I'm sure they are fine," he answered. "I'm not really concerned. I cannot remember many women in my life who were ever on time. A chipped nail, a hair out of place, a little rouge—you know how women are."

This seemed to satisfy Perrin and he and Masters then sauntered over to where the Senator was seated in his unusual chair, surrounded by his three-man escort and Martin. "Senator Danton, I'm happy to see you have recovered somewhat from the effects of the storm. How do you feel?"

"I feel like Hell, but that doesn't concern me at the moment. Do you know what the Sam Hill is going on here—and where the Sam Hill we are?"

"Not yet, Senator, but that fellow Nikto has promised some answers later on."

Their chat was interrupted by a low wolf whistle. Masters turned to see that Sim and Helen Barron, together with Tiffany and Jennifer, had stepped out into the hall almost simultaneously. He was inclined to follow suit on that whistle. Barron, of course, was dressed as he was, but the women—well, that was something else again.

They wore identical short, pale green tunics over sheer hose of the same color. The tunics were hemmed with a dark green band and had collars and cuffs to match. Their high-heeled boots were also of the pale green color, and reached mid-calf to end in a cuff of the darker green.

They did not, however, have much time to admire the ladies for, as soon as everyone was in the corridor, the several soldiers on the level started to gather the passengers together. It appeared that it was time for dinner. The soldiers directed them into the downward shaft. Masters once again felt that ever-so-slight moving sensation, then was propelled gently outward. This must be the level at which they entered the ship, he thought. Earlier they had moved up one level and now they had moved down one level. He really could not tell since all the levels around the shafts were identical. They were directed to an open doorway where Nikto stood waiting for them.

Inside was a large buffet table with every food imaginable and some that were not so imaginable. There were several small tables and chairs set up and Nikto indicated that they should commence.

Well, thought Masters, now is no time to hesitate and so led the way to the large table.

He ate ravenously of the foods he had chosen, finding them to be quite tasty. As he leaned back in his chair after the meal, enjoying what was a close substitute for coffee, he actually found himself enjoying the situation he was in. He had wanted a little adventure on this trip, hadn't he? Well, here it was and there was nothing he could, or in fact wanted to, do about it for the moment so he might as well make the best of it and enjoy what he could.

The meal passed without incident and now Nikto made an announcement that, though the ship was approaching Encandor, all passengers would be quartered in the ship for the night, and tomorrow any questions they might have would be answered.

Somewhat disappointed, they trooped back to the Access Shaft. Well, thought Masters, this is going to be a ver-r-r-y long night.

*   *   *

Davis opened his eyes to total darkness. He could feel the slight swaying motion of the boat. His head ached and his eyes felt gritty.

Memory flooded back. My God, what an experience! He had watched Masters as he left the wheelhouse, thinking that the worst of the storm was over. In actuality, it had just begun.

A dull roar, then a deafening sound, had drawn his attention away from the door and the retreating Masters. He turned just in time to see a tower of white water that reached beyond the sky bearing down on the yacht. Suddenly, the night was brighter than day; so bright the light hurt his eyes. As suddenly as it had come, it was gone. His eyes were just becoming accustomed to the dim light when he realized that the yacht had taken on speed and yawed dangerously to port. It was all he could do to keep his balance. The air in the small, cramped quarters was thick and it was hard to breathe. The boat leveled, then rolled to starboard. He had just a second to see what was happening and was instantly sorry that he did. He had looked into the heart of Hell, down into the Well of Hades, darker than night, and The Seeker was perched just on the brink.

He felt a momentary rush of nausea as his mind whirled with the memory of that awful nightmare. He remembered the waves crashing over the boat, threatening to capsize it; peering down into that awful hole and the bow of the boat dipping dangerously low as it started to slide into the chasm created by the swirling waters; and, worst of all, The Seeker suspended in mid-air—just hanging in the sky; then the plummet downward to land in the water, nearly swamping the boat.

His eyes riveted on the action, he had instinctively reached for the bottle of whisky always near at hand. His hand encountered broken glass. He felt a twinge of pain and pulled back his hand. Blood! What rotten luck! Well, what had he expected, anyway?

He reached for the intercom. "Cliff! Bill!" No answer. "Anyone?" His cries went unheeded; unanswered. In the eerie half-light, he had left the wheelhouse and carefully made his way aft. As he started down the ladder, he saw Masters at the bottom, crumpled in a heap like a rag doll. "Masters?" His voice was no longer strident, authoritative; rather, it was timid, unsure. Again, "Masters?"

Unwilling to touch, for fear that he was dead, Davis gingerly stepped over Masters' body and opened the first stateroom door he reached. It was Senator Danton's room. The Senator was lying on his bed and his body appeared to be drained of all blood. His aide, Martin, was slumped over the edge of the bed, one arm reaching toward the Senator as though he had been trying to help him.

Oh, my God, he thought. I have killed them all. May God forgive me. I really didn't mean to do it. His mind could not stand the pain and guilt. Numbly, he retreated from the Senator's room and carefully made his way forward and down to his own quarters. Without actual realization, he took a bottle from the cupboard and, hugging it close to his chest, he sidled down the narrow passageway to the engine room and back to a remote corner where he could have his own private thoughts. His own private dreams. His own private Hell.

He woke to a slight rocking of the boat. His first thought was of the passengers and crew. He recalled his last sight of them. The memory sobered him. There was no sound in the darkness. Darkness? Why WAS it so dark? There should be SOME light, even in this corner. Carefully, he rose to his feet and inched his way along the bulkhead to the door. Opening it just a crack, he saw a pale light ahead and started toward it.

As he entered the passageway, he heard voices ahead and a feeling of elation came over him. He had not killed them after all. He quickened his pace and was just about to yell when one of the voices called out in a language unfamiliar to him. He stopped immediately. What was going on? He edged forward. The voices were still not loud enough to understand but they were coming closer. He backed up into the shadows just as two men in strange blue uniforms walked by, apparently chatting amiably, but in a strange language.

He waited until they were well out of sight, then, his curiosity peaked, he decided to investigate a little. He followed the sound of the voices through the crews' quarters, up the ladder, down the passageway which led to the passengers' cabins, and then up onto the deck. He neither saw nor heard anyone else. When he arrived on deck himself, he immediately noted that the yacht was tied up to a pier. How had that happened? Had the Coast Guard found them after all? But, then, who were these strangers?

He had just started making a visual survey when he again heard voices. He ducked down the ladder just as the two men he had been following returned from a tour of the deck. After they passed by, he stepped back to the deck. He watched them as they strolled down the gangway, onto the pier, and toward a building which appeared to be some sort of warehouse.

He waited until they entered the building, all the while listening carefully for any sound of others who might be on the yacht. Hearing only the familiar sounds of the boat and the water, and so feeling more at ease, he quickly retraced his steps to the passenger section and lightly rapped on Perrin's door. No answer. He tried again, then tried the knob. It opened easily but a cursory glance told him the cabin was empty. He moved on down the passageway to the next door. That cabin was empty also. The same scene greeted him in all the staterooms—neat and orderly, but no one around.

The crew! If they were alive, some of the crew must be on board. He took the steps of the ladder two at a time. "Cliff! Skip!" The words rang through the empty air. He modulated his voice to a throaty whisper. "Bob! Fred!" He checked each room; each bunk. No one on board!

Concern creased his forehead. His heart began to race. He leaned back against the bulkhead and forced himself to relax. There must be a logical explanation. Since they were in port, if the crew and passengers were alive, possibly all had gone ashore. His heart stopped pounding. He wanted to believe they were alive and well. That must be it: they had all gone ashore. Now that he had it settled in his mind, he went topside to check what port this actually might be.

Upon reaching the deck, he first checked the skyline, but found it totally unfamiliar. This was not too surprising. There were many ports in this part of the North Atlantic he had never been in; this must be one of them. But … how did they make a port so quickly? They were out in the middle of the ocean. Could the storm have blown them so far in so short a time? That was unlikely, even as strong as the winds were.

He climbed the ladder to the wheelhouse to check the stars and, although he saw a few faint ones, due to the light from the pier, it was impossible to get any kind of fix. It was in his mind to check out the pier itself when a beam of light interrupted his thoughts. It was the door to the warehouse building and the two men were coming out. They started down the pier toward the yacht.

He descended the ladder to the deck. They were still coming this way. He looked quickly around the deck. No safe place here. He made his way down the ladder and through the passenger section, then paused. He would wait here and see. Perhaps those men would go back to the warehouse and give him a chance to get a better look at the pier and the surrounding area. He listened for a long moment, then a sudden thought struck him…there was really no point taking chances at night, and especially in a strange port. He could always check it out tomorrow when it was light … it would be safer then. Also, the crew must surely return in the morning. With that settled in his mind, he dashed on down the companionway to his quarters, where the dark and the whisky provided a comparatively safe, and definitely warm, haven.

*   *   *

There was a knock on the door.

"Enter."

"Mistress, I have news. A small boat has come through the Eye of Balim. There are just a few persons but some you might find interesting."

Naila looked at Nantu, one of her father's personal guards. "Why might I find otherworlders interesting?"

"One is said to be a handsome dark-haired giant and there is a woman said to be 'fit for the Altar of Balim.'"

"Where are they now?"

"Still on the ship commanded by Nikto. He thought to keep them there overnight until it could be decided what D'Ar wished to have done with them.

"I would see these two now; however, I wish to do so without Nikto's knowledge."

As they walked down the corridor toward the hangar, Naila thought about Nikto. He was a soldier in the service of her father and had worked his way up to the highest possible position in the Temple Guard and was much admired by D'Ar. Even so, Nikto did not approve of the Temple sacrifices and, at times, had bordered on insubordination when he was required to participate in certain of the ceremonies. There had been some talk of an Alliance between Nikto and herself. It was certainly no secret that Nikto was ambitious and would welcome such an Alliance; however, she saw no particular advantage to herself. To her, he was but a useful tool to gain what she wished— nothing more. If and when the time came for her to take a mate, she would decide about Nikto and she also would make her own choice of a mate.

By this time they had reached the ship and Nantu took her first to see the woman—actually, there were two; one with short blond hair and one with long dark hair. Neither awakened at her entry and she stood silently for some time appraising first one, then the other. There were possibilities of using both—her mind was working overtime as she recounted to herself the various ways in which she might use these women.

Next they went to see the man. Again, here, there were two but the tall dark-haired one was superb. And, he had facial hair. Most unusual as no man on Encandor had such. There was no question in her mind what she wanted to do with this one. All she must do now is get around her father but that would be easily done—he had yet to refuse her anything.

"What...? Oh, is it morning already?" Masters felt a hand on his shoulder. It was with great difficultly that he opened his eyes. He had spent a good deal of the night tossing, turning, pacing, and when he finally slept it was the sleep of sheer exhaustion. Now it was morning; at least he assumed it was. There was really no way he could tell unless he could get outside this sphere. He managed to get his eyes open enough to look at his watch—5:00—in the morning. In the morning? What an ungodly hour. His eyes closed involuntarily.

Someone was shaking him again. "Reg, wake up." He opened his eyes again to see Perrin's back. Perrin was perched on the edge of the bed and staring in the direction of the door.

Masters raised up on one elbow and his eyes followed Perrin's gaze. A woman? Here? In his quarters? At 5:00 a.m.? But, what a woman! She was a vision in a dream. He rubbed his eyes, then looked again. Maybe it wasn't a dream after all. She was undoubtedly the most beautiful woman he had ever seen. Alabaster skin glowed through fine netting of royal blue which covered her arms. The low-cut bodice of her dress was tightly fitted and a navy blue panel ran from neckline to floor in front and joined to side panels of the netting to form a skirt where shapely legs were evident on either side of the panel. She wore high-healed sandals of what appeared to be malleable silver. A silver tiara, topped by an intricate carving of the circle and triangle insignia, crowned her honey-colored hair, which was piled high on top of her head with several ringlets on either side reaching down to her shoulders. Her cool blue eyes appraised him carefully.

Masters watched her gaze with an appraisal of his own. "We-e-ell, good morning. And what may we do for you?"

She gave no indication whatever that she had heard, or even understood, his question but turned instead to the soldier who had accompanied her and nodded. He bowed in acknowledgement of whatever secret they held between them, and the two quickly left the room. This was going to be even more interesting than he had hoped, mused Masters to himself.

"What was all that?" Perrin mumbled and looked at Masters.

"Damned if I know."

SACRIFICE!

A tiny finger of golden sunlight poked at copper curls cascading over the satin pillow and traced a lazy trail down one ivory cheek. Leila lifted a delicately carved hand and brushed at the light to no avail. She turned over and tried unsuccessfully to bury her head in the pillow. Lifting herself up on one elbow, she searched through sleepy eyes for some way to shut out the sun; finding none, she dropped back to her pillow.

Somehow, the nights were never quite long enough. And especially last night. She had tossed and turned for hours and had finally gotten to sleep just before dawn. She tried to go back to sleep but the memory of yesterday nagged at her like a toothache.

She heard the Morning Chimes, shook her head to clear it of the unpleasant thoughts, and rose from her bed. Standing as high as she could on the tips of her toes, she clasped her hands, took a deep breath and stretched her arms upward as far as she could reach, then relaxed. It felt good. She quickly showered and went to the Common Room for the morning meal with her sister and father. She would have been pleased to skip this morning, but it was a tradition of her father for as long as she could remember, and her father ruled his household as he ruled his world—Encandor. Her father was D'Ar, High Priest of Balim.

It had been said that D'Ar was High Priest of Balim when the sun was white and hot. She thought this to be an exaggeration, for it was recorded in the Great Books of the Temple that he took Oath in the Fifteenth Dakar of Mesto, his predecessor, and this was now the Tenth Dakar of D'Ar.

A most imposing man, D'Ar ruled Encandor with an iron hand. Iltarn, Emperor by succession, had become merely a figurehead. By pandering to Iltarn's lascivious nature, D'Ar gained a free hand with regard to all matters of the Temple, and thereby controlled the Empire.

"Good Morn, Leila. May Balim take delight in you this day."

"Good Morn, Naila. May Balim take delight in YOU this day."

Naila was her senior by one dakar and found much favor in D'Ar's eyes.

By Temple Law, the High Priest is forbidden the right to heirs, either male or female. But, so powerful was her father, that he had taken Maora, a Virgin of Balim, to wife. She bore him a daughter, Naila, in the first year, then was without child until the birth of Leila. Maora's spirit returned to Balim with the birth of her second daughter.

D'Ar had so loved Maora that he offered his spirit to Balim in her stead, but it was not to be so. As her spirit began its long journey, D'Ar swore to elevate her firstborn above all men. Never before had a woman served Balim at the Altar other than as sacrifice to the god.

D'Ar honored his oath to Maora and elevated Naila to the position of High Priestess and Initiate in the Ancient Secrets and Leila he appointed as Keeper of the Flame of Balim.

"There will be an Audience today." Her thoughts were interrupted by Naila's smug statement.

"Why? I have heard nothing of this."

"Nantu reported a new arrival to me last night. One is a dark-haired giant. I have seen him." There was just a trace of excitement in her voice. Leila wondered how Nikto might feel about this should he hear. It was common knowledge that he and her father had looked favorably upon an Alliance between Naila and Nikto. She wondered now if perhaps Naila had something else in mind. It would not be the first time she disputed her father's authority and, ultimately, he always gave in to her wishes and whims of the moment.

Further speculation was impossible as D'Ar entered the room at that moment and the meal commenced.

There was little conversation during the meal and for this Leila was secretly glad. D'Ar seemed preoccupied and stayed only long enough to complete the meal and Naila left immediately after with the excuse that she must ready herself for the Audience, which was to be held one hour past midday.

Realizing that she, too, must prepare for the Audience, but reluctant to don her formal attire this early, Leila thought she might get a look at the new arrival of whom Naila spoke so warmly. Her mind made up, she started toward the quarters where the strangers were usually kept and, without thinking, cut through the Great Hall. As she opened the door, memory flooded her mind. Suddenly, in her mind's eye, it was yesterday!

*   *   *

No sound was to be heard in the Great Hall of the Temple though it was crowded. Leila surveyed the scene through lacy curtains, which only partially shielded her from the worshipers. Her eyes searched the room. There were long benches, filled to capacity, lining either side of a wide strip of crimson carpet running from the door across the room and up a long stairway leading to the Altar of Balim. High above the altar was an imposing statue of Balim, the one-eyed god, some twenty feet high.

Leila had always found the Day of Sacrifice most distasteful and today she was to have carried the Flame of Balim to the altar. She had even donned her gown for the ceremony. It was of the palest blue silk and hugged her body like a dream. It had a stand-up collar that formed a vee at her throat; her shoulders were completely bare. The bodice was fitted and ended in an ankle-length straight skirt which was slit on the left side to the thigh. She had begged to be excused, but only at the last moment had D'Ar relented and excused her from participation; however, he had ordered her to attend and observe.

She was startled when she heard the gong heralding the commencement of the ceremonies. She turned toward the door to see two young girls about fifteen years of age enter the Hall and proceed toward the stairs. Each wore a plain white floor-length robe with scoop neck and long, flowing sleeves. One carried an alabaster bowl partially filled with an amber-colored liquid and had a linen towel draped over one arm. The other carried the Flame of Balim.

Her eyes move on to the next in line. It must be a Virgin of Balim since there had been no otherworlders for ever so long. Oh, no! Not Kiera! Leila was shocked and saddened to see her best friend following the girls. She was barefoot and dressed in the sacrificial robe, which consisted of a collar of precious gems of many colors and shapes from which hung many strands of the gems reaching to the tips of her breasts. Her skirt was of the same stones, but in strands flowing from hip to floor and made a tinkling sound as she walked. Kiera, now twenty, had been offered to Balim at birth and had resided all her life in the House of Balim. She had long been resigned to her fate as a Virgin of Balim, but Leila had hoped that she could dissuade D'Ar from this most unpleasant custom before Kiera's time had come.

Perhaps D'Ar was using this as a punishment for her obstinacy earlier but, in actuality, she could see Naila's fine hand in this choice, for her father was quite fond of Kiera and, too, she was not due to be the Bride of Balim for yet another year.

Tear-dimmed eyes sadly followed her friend until she reached the foot of the stairs.

The gong sounded again and all eyes returned to the door as Naila entered the Hall, head held high. She was wearing tight silver pants with an overskirt from the waist similar to that which Kiera wore, but of silver beads rather than gems. The top, a silver lamé scarf, began at the waist on the left side, moved upward to cover her left breast and looped around her throat to form a collar of sorts, then down the other side, covering the other breast, to end at the waist on the right side. Silver sandals completed her costume. A tiara of silver with the Temple emblem topped her upswept curls. In her hands, she carried a plain silver tray.

Naila luxuriated in the attention she gained from her position; and today she was accorded a new honor. She was to preside with D'Ar for the first time. It was almost a certainty that Naila would be chosen by D'Ar to take Oath upon his passing and rule Encandor in her own right. At the present there was none to stand in her way. Her gaze scanned the room until it came to rest on the curtain behind which Leila had secreted herself. Leila saw a triumphant gleam of satisfaction and a hint of a smile before Naila turned her gaze forward once again. She had not missed a single step on her way to the bloody altar which was waiting to receive Leila's lifetime friend.

Following Naila came D'Ar, clad in a plain crimson robe. As he approached the stairs, the worshipers genuflected.

By Temple records, D'Ar started the practice of blood sacrifice in the Seventh Dakar of his reign. It was at that time Balim first opened his Eye and looked with favor upon D'Ar and drew him up to his bosom. The people of Encandor stood in awe of the only high priest so honored by Balim and dared not oppose him. The sacrifices increased and Balim continued to favor his most faithful servant.

After one such occurrence, the Strangers appeared in Encandor and D'Ar told the people this was a sign from Balim and that, from hence, Balim himself would provide the sacrificial victims for his altar. But, of late, Balim had furnished no victims and D'Ar admonished his people and told them that their faith was growing thin and that Balim demanded a Virgin Bride.

By this time, the two young girls had reached the top of the stairs and were standing at the foot of the altar. Kiera was lying on the altar looking upward at the statue of Balim. On the altar beside her head lay a long-bladed knife with an ornately carved and jeweled hilt.

Naila stood at the head of the altar.

D'Ar ascended the last step and stood before the statue of Balim with arms outstretched in supplication. "Balim, Great God, we ask that you accept this pure heart in your honor." He turned to the altar, picked up the knife with both hands on the hilt, raised it high above his head. "From this day hence, Kiera, you are and ever will be, the Bride of Balim." He plunged the knife deep into her breast. As the blade struck home, Leila saw her friend's body convulse, then become still. There was a low murmur from the crowded room as a small fountain of blood sprayed upward. Though Kiera made no sound, in her mind Leila heard screams from the past of those not so brave or dedicated as her friend.

Leila's face remained frozen and, while her pain and emotion did not show, a single tear traced it's way down one lovely cheek.

With great precision—that which comes from years of practice—D'Ar deftly cut the heart from Kiera's breast and placed it on the silver tray. He then moved to the foot of the altar and washed his hands in the amber liquid and dried them on the linen towel. This completed, he nodded imperceptibly to Naila. Carrying the tray, she met him mid-altar and they proceeded together to the smaller altar beneath the statue of Balim. There, D'Ar opened a panel in the front of the altar and, when Naila had placed the tray inside, he closed it. Surreptitiously, he took a small key from the pocket of his robe and inserted it into a slot to the right of the panel.

While this was being done, the two young girls moved to the altar and removed the ceremonial costume from Kiera. After completing this task, one of them depressed a small button on the side of the altar and both stepped back. The altar slab began slowly to descend inside the base until the body disappeared completely.

"Balim, Great God," D'Ar intoned, "show us your acceptance of this sacrifice. Let the mighty gales blow; let the waters rise up from their depths   even to thc sky; put your lens of darkness over the face of the sun; open your Eye and let your light shine upon our world. Balim, Great God, bring us new offerings for your altar. Balim, Great God, show us your power!"

He turned the key. Immediately, a swirl of multicolored mist rose from the floor and enveloped D'Ar and Naila and as it rose toward the ceiling, they appeared to be borne upward along with it. It rose until the two were at eye-level with the statue of the god. Then, as quickly as it had come, it dispersed and D'Ar and Naila were once again standing before the Altar of Balim.

Without the Temple, the winds began to rise and the sun darkened. Leila had never witnessed it herself, but there were those who had, and had told her that the waters did indeed rise from their depths, and Balim most certainly did open his Eye— they had seen the great light. Some of those who had looked upon the Eye of Balim, were they close enough, had never again seen the things of this world. Some even, those who found not favor with the god, had died most horrible deaths. D'Ar proclaimed that those who had seen the Eye of Balim and had died, had perished because of lack of faith in their god.

With tearful eyes, Leila had quitted the hall and repaired to her apartments to grieve for her friend.

The bells rang Midday. Leila forced herself back to the present, wiped the tears from her eyes, and left the hall. Naila had said there would be an Audience today and she had less than an hour to prepare. She went directly to her apartments to don her ceremonial gown, then to the audience chamber where D'Ar and Naila were already waiting.

*   *   *

Masters did not have much time to puzzle out this mystery as they were shortly summoned to the morning meal. Breakfast passed uneventfully and ever so slowly. He was anxious to get it over with and see what he could find out about this place, and what they could expect in the future.

Just as he finished with his meal, Nikto came up to his table. "You will please accompany me."

"Just where are you taking me?"

"You have been summoned by the High Priestess Naila."

"High Priestess Naila? Who the HELL is she? AND, what exactly is going on here? I want some answers NOW." This whole affair had gotten out of hand. He stopped dead in his tracks. "I'm not budging until I get some answers. And, how is it you speak our language? What about my friends? What's to become of…?"

Nikto held up his hand for silence. "Your questions will be answered by the High Priestess herself. For now, your friends are to be taken to the Temple where you will join them later."

"The Temple?"

"The Temple of Balim. We are soldiers in the service of D'Ar, High Priest of Balim."

High Priestess? High Priest? Temple? It smacked of good old-fashioned paganism … but the technology of these people—at least what he had seen so far—certainly gave the lie to that. If nothing else, this was going to be an interesting adventure.

He rose from the table and followed Nikto from the room. They moved down one of the four corridors. By this time he had lost all sense of direction and, when they reached the end of the corridor, Nikto pressed one of the studs on his belt and the side of the ship opened up as it had yesterday. Only this time there was no water. Instead, he found that they were inside what appeared to be a hangar. The ship was "docked" in a deep depression so that the flange or stabilizer was resting on the pad. There were spaces for other ships, but none were in evidence at the moment.

Looking around him, Masters thought of The Seeker and her captain who, he hoped, was still aboard. He wondered how far away they were and in what direction. He carefully took note of all he saw. One could never be too careful and, until he knew exactly what was going on, no information was too trivial to note. It might come in handy later on.

They soon reached the nearest wall of the hangar and Nikto again fingered another of the studs on his belt. As the doorway opened for them, Masters thought that this explained at least a couple of the studs on Nikto's belt-they apparently were electronic keys. He wondered if all were keys, but decided to await a more propitious moment before questioning Nikto about the mechanics of his world.

They walked through the doorway and came into a long hallway with several doors on either side. Nikto passed several of the doors and came to a stop before one emblazoned with the circle and triangle. There he knocked lightly.

"Enter."

It was a woman's voice and when Nikto opened the door, Masters recognized the possessor as the woman he had seen in his quarters earlier. She was standing by an overstuffed chair, one of several that were placed around a small round table. There was a soft glow emanating from the walls, which provided the only lighting. If this was an interrogation room, it was the strangest he had ever seen.

Nikto made a curt bow. "This is the one called Masters." Then, turning to Masters, "My Mistress Naila, High Priestess of Balim." He made another small bow and left the room.

"Please sit." Her voice had the quality of wind chimes in a soft, summer breeze. With only a trace of a smile, she indicated one of several glasses that were on the small table. Masters waved his refusal.

"What I would LIKE are some answers. I think we've waited long enough." His voice was curt and demanding.

"What is it you wish to know?"

"Where we are, for one thing."

"Why, Encandor, of course."

This was more than a little exasperating. "We KNOW it's Encandor! Nikto told us that! But where the HELL IS Encandor and WHERE ARE WE?"

His voice was harsher than he had intended and he saw a tiny frown wrinkle her forehead. "YOU WILL NOT SPEAK THUS TO THE HIGH PRIESTESS OF BALIM." As warm and musical as her voice had been previously, it was now frosty and brittle. She put her fingers to her throat. "Nikto!" It was hardly more than a whisper.

Nikto opened the door and Naila dismissed Masters with a wave of her hand. What a sorry mess! And just when he might have gotten some information. He really blew this one.

"We'll take an aircar to the Temple." Nikto led the way as they walked further on down the hallway and away from the hangar. They arrived shortly at an intersecting corridor where several small vehicles were parked.

Nikto directed Masters to a vehicle that was large enough for only the two of them. It contained a double seat in the rear and a panel of buttons in front. When Nikto was seated beside Masters, he punched out a code on the panel. The vehicle lifted into the air approximately two feet and moved rapidly forward. It continued on a straight course for several minutes, then stopped in what appeared to be a large station where he saw several more of the small aircars, together with some larger versions, apparently used for conveying several passengers at one time.

They left the aircar and proceeded up a wide stairway, across a hallway and into a small reception room. "Your friends are here." He indicated a door. "I think you will find the accommodations most satisfactory." With this he turned to go, leaving a still somewhat dejected Masters standing alone in the middle of the room.

*   *   *

Nikto frowned slightly as he left Masters. This was a new development. Never before had Naila shown such an interest in any of the strangers. It continued to annoy him, though he tried to shake the feeling. He was uncertain just what kind of feeling it was or what it meant. Though D'Ar had openly spoken of an Alliance between him and Naila, she made no indication that such was her desire. He would find an Alliance with Naila to be pleasant and gratifying in many ways but Naila's thirst for the blood sacrifices was not at all to his liking.

His footsteps involuntarily carried him to an observation station behind the strangers' quarters. Absentmindedly, he set the controls on the panel and flipped the switch.

He was momentarily taken aback at the picture on the screen. It certainly was not what he had expected to see. The girl was standing in the middle of the room, opening admiring her nude body in the many mirrors adorning the walls. He had not intended to spy, but now he could not take his eyes from her. She was caressing her body with slender, delicate hands. Her long dark hair swung out from her body as she stood on tiptoes and whirled about in a savage little dance. This continued for a moment or so, then she fell to her knees, legs spread wide, threw up her arms and leaned backward, her body slowly undulating back and forth, back and forth. He felt a sudden desire in his loins such as he had not felt before. Then, as though she knew he was watching her, she looked upward and stared, unabashed, directly into his face. Although he knew it was impossible for her to see him, he was embarrassed, as much for his desire as for watching, and immediately shut off the camera.

Who was this creature? Certainly, she must be one of the strangers. There were not too many but, somehow, he must have missed her when she boarded. Her life, however, would be most uncertain once she had been seen by Naila.

He was now overcome with an anger such as he had never before experienced. He knew that this one most certainly would grace the Altar of Balim if Naila had the power—and she did. He now swore a silent oath that this would not happen. By his life, IT WOULD NOT HAPPEN!

It was with new determination that he strode from the chamber and went about his duties.

AUDIENCE

"When the High Priest enters, you will all bow thus." The speaker was a young man, apparently in his thirties, and was demonstrating a shallow bow from the waist. "You will remain in this position until he has mounted the steps and turned to face forward."

Masters watched him distractedly. Earlier, when he had entered the door Nikto had indicated, he had indeed found the quarters to be "quite" satisfactory. In fact, he had entered into an enormous common room which was furnished as richly and tastefully as any of the plush hotels in which he had ever stayed. Directly across the room was a wide hallway and on either side of this were two bedrooms equal in furnishings to the common room.

He soon learned that he was sharing these quarters with Alex Perrin, Sim Barron and Donald Martin. The Senator, Martin had told him, was put in the custody of a physician and taken to a "hospital" or "clinic," although they did not call it that.

He also learned that Helen Barron, along with Jennifer and Tiffany, had apparently been taken to a women's section, and the crew, including Charley, were in the area next door to them.

Upon checking the door, he found that it was unlocked and they were presumably free to come and go as they pleased. Perrin and his companions, however, were informed before Masters arrived that they would be called shortly to appear before the High Priest, and it was suggested that they wait in their chambers until after the Audience, at which time they would be conducted on a tour of the entire complex should they so desire.

And so, they were all together again; learning how to comport themselves in the presence of the High Priest in a very large room not unlike a hotel lobby, but without a registration desk. There were overstuffed chairs and marble benches set amidst rich hangings of various shades of blue, some in velvet and others in faille interlaced with silver and with panels of blue chiffon interspersed in between.

To his right he could see where a large niche had been cut into the wall. Heavy draperies flanked either side. There were two steps leading up to a wide dais on which rested a large ornate silver chair or throne. Resting on a pedestal rising from the center back was the now familiar symbol. On either side was a smaller chair. All three had navy blue velvet cushions and backs. Leading up to the dais and across the marble floor was a wide runner of navy blue, deep-pile carpet.

Masters glanced at the rest of the group. They appeared to be adjusting somewhat to the situation. At least there did not appear to be the great concern and apprehension that was visible at their first contact with these strange, new people.

The droning voice stopped and the young man motioned the group into position to the right of the carpet runner; the women in front, Masters, Perrin, Barron and Martin forming a second line, and the crew members in back of them. The senator had not been returned to the group. His whereabouts and well-being were first on Master's list once they were permitted to ask questions.

Upon hearing a commotion to his left, Masters turned to see six or seven men of various ages and in brightly colored robes enter the room and move to a position just opposite them. Then came four soldiers in royal blue uniforms, who took up their positions—two on either side of the dais.

Close on their heels came Nikto, who stood just to the right and slightly forward of Masters' group. He turned to face the door. "Leila, Guardian of the Flame of Balim," he announced.

Coming toward them, dressed in a plain, caftan-like robe of royal blue velvet with silver borders, was a near duplicate of his lady of the evening, except for her hair which, though blond, had a definite copper tone, and at about five foot three appeared to be some two or three inches shorter. She proceeded up the steps to the dais and turned to stand in front of the small chair on the left-hand side of the throne.

"Naila, High Priestess of Balim and Initiate in the Ancient Mysteries."

Here, now, was his lady of last night and his interview of this morning. She was dressed in a navy blue silk robe shot through with silver and of a design similar to that of the other. She, too, stepped up on the dais and turned to stand in front of the other small chair. Each woman wore a silver tiara which bore the Temple emblem.

"D'Ar, High Priest of Balim, Keeper of the Ancient Secrets, and Spiritual Ruler of Encandor."

About twenty paces behind the women came a stately man, who appeared to be in his sixties. He was of the same complexion and coloring as the women. He wore a navy blue robe devoid of decoration and, in his right hand, he carried a silver scepter which bore the circle and triangle.

He walked slowly toward the stairs, looking neither right nor left, stepped up to the dais, turned, and sat on the throne. He waited until the two women were seated and then addressed himself to his audience.

"It is well that you should know that you can never return to the world you knew."

Here he paused, as though to let them become aware of the full portent of his statement. A slight murmur ran through the group and Sim Barron reached forward to put his hand on his wife's shoulder.

"The phenomenon which opens the portal and which permitted your entry into our world, allows entry only. There has been no occasion to the contrary.

"We understand your reluctance to accept this as fact. It is always difficult to leave one's home; but to be faced with the knowledge that one can never return presents a thesis totally unacceptable to the rational mind.

"We here in Encandor would be your friends and brothers. In return, we ask only that you permit us to learn more of your world.

"It is conceivable to us that you, too, might wish to learn. In anticipation of such a desire on your part, guides have been assigned who will acquaint you with our customs, our laws, our people, and our city.

"For the present, you shall be treated as honored guests."

So stunned were they at this pronouncement, it was several moments before the group realized that the Audience was at an end and by this time the High Priest and his retinue were well on their way out of the room.

*   *   *

Leila took her place in the procession as it began. She could hear Nikto announce her arrival as she entered the chamber. Secretly, she glanced at the new arrivals to see if she could pick out the one of whom Naila had spoken. There he was! Her eyes sought his, but at that moment Nikto announced Naila and the stranger turned towards her, admiration showing in his eyes. Leila was smote by a sudden pang of jealousy, which she quickly smothered. She had not even met him. She proceeded on up the dais and took her place.

She continued to watch the strangers during D'Ar's proclamation, and determined that she would be the one to guide this man on a tour of Encandor. She realized, however, that this might not be an easy task, as Naila had definitely shown an interest in this man earlier. Perhaps Nikto would be able to help her. She would seek him out as soon as the ceremony was ended.

At the conclusion of the ceremonies, Nikto led the strangers out of the hall and back to their quarters. He had explained to them that the tours of which D'Ar had spoken would be arranged for and occur early the following morning. This evening, however, they were to be left to their own devices other than the evening meal for which they would be summoned. Now, he was on his way back to the Temple proper.

"Nikto."

He stopped and turned.

"Nikto, stop and hold for a moment." Leila was rushing towards him. "I have a favor I would ask."

Nikto laughed lightly. "And what could the small one wish of me."

"I would lead a tour tomorrow."

"You know it is forbidden by D'Ar."

"D'Ar would not have to know, would he?"

"You ask a great deal, Leila."

"I know you can do it, Nikto. You have done it before."

And this was true. Nikto had, on several occasions, allowed Leila to conduct one of the several tours when the strangers had come to Encandor. This time, however, she seemed somewhat more excited than she had on previous occasions. And he was rather reluctant to give in to her whims.

"You know that the risk runs high each time you step into the streets."

"Nikto, please. I would guide the tall dark-haired one tomorrow."

And now he knew the reason for her excitement. Perhaps he would do it just this one time again, for he had remembered how Naila had looked at this "dark-haired giant" when she had seen him earlier this morning. Perhaps he could use Leila's desire to suit his own purposes.

He had little to gain and much to lose just by letting Leila go out into the streets of Encandor—more so with an otherworlder. However, though it might not ultimately thwart Naila's purposes, his personal irritation with her goaded him into taking a risk with Leila not particularly to his liking. True, she had gone on tours before, but never had she been interested in a particular person.

She now looked at him expectantly, with pleading in her eyes. His attitude toward her was that of an older brother and she looked so pathetic, so he smiled. "Well, small one, it appears that this is your lucky day. It seems that I am short one tour guide, and I see no reason why you should not guide the dark-haired one as well as any other."

Leila stood on tiptoes to reach up and hug him around the neck. He lifted her completely off the floor, swung her around in a circle, then placed her back on her feet. She immediately rushed away to savor her good fortune.

Nikto continued on toward the Temple, slightly troubled at what he had done; then shrugged his shoulders and brushed the thought from his mind. If he were lucky as before, neither D'Ar nor Naila would learn of Leila's escapades.

Leila fairly danced down the hallway on her way back to her apartments. She had decided to skip the evening meal and go to bed early, so that she would be well rested for the morning when she would meet the handsome stranger. In her present excitement, all thoughts of the previous day and her friend were washed from her mind.

She spent many long moments making faces at the image in her mirror; practicing just what she would say and imagining what he might say in return; and reflecting on the proper attitude befitting the daughter of D'Ar—the daughter of D'Ar who was sneaking out of the Temple for a rendezvous with a total, albeit handsome, stranger.

*   *   *

It was barely an hour since the Audience had ended. Donald Martin had gone back to Senator Danton and Masters, Perrin, and Sim Barron had wandered through the building together trying to figure out what some objects represented, admiring others, and speculating on the type of people the Encandorians might be.

They had inspected what obviously was a place of worship—it contained an altar and a gigantic statue of a cyclops. It was somewhat of a surprise to see something familiar (even though only a myth at home) in this place where NOTHING was familiar. It even gave Masters a fleeting sense of security, however small.

The trio sauntered back to the living quarters, where the crew of The Seeker were playing a game of cards. Masters could only guess where they had found a deck of cards but was glad that they had something with which to occupy their minds and keep them from thinking too much on what had occurred earlier. He was shaken up quite a bit himself by the discourse and could well imagine what was going on in the minds of the others.

He could not understand, however, why the men were separated from the women. Sim was especially feeling this because he was greatly concerned for Helen. The guards had literally pulled them apart after the ceremony and dragged a softly sobbing Helen out with Jennifer and Tiffany while the men stood helplessly by. Masters had asked Nikto for a special consideration in this regard but Nikto had said Temple Rules forbade those men and women living in the Temple to mingle or cohabitate whether or not there was an Alliance between any two of them. And, according to Nikto, Temple Rules MUST be obeyed. There were no exceptions.

The rest of the day passed without incident and Masters retired early.

*   *   *

Leila rose at the First Chime, hurriedly dressed and went down to breakfast, hoping that D'Ar and Naila would already be there, and have nothing planned for her to do this day. As it turned out, D'Ar had a very important errand for Naila, and was himself on his way to a conference with the lesser priests and so dismissed Leila quickly, which suited her purposes well.

Rushing back to her apartments, she changed into a pale green robe of the working class and went immediately to the audience chamber where Nikto would have the strangers gathered for assignment of guides.

She arrived just as he had assigned the last of the guides and thought perhaps he had forgotten his promise to her, as the handsome stranger was nowhere in sight. Crestfallen, she determined to make the best of it.

"Nikto, good morn. May Balim smile on you this day."

Nikto turned and, seeing her sad appearance, chuckled. "Good morn, small one. May Balim smile on you this day."

"Nikto," she began—hesitated—then continued, "do you remember not your promises?"

"I remember. Come with me."

He led her to a small doorway to the right of the dais and pressed one of the studs on his belt. When the door opened, he took her by the hand and led her into the room beyond. There Masters was waiting.

"Masters, this is my Mistress Leila who will be your guide today." The introduction complete, he stepped back through the door, which closed behind him.

Masters looked at Leila with an appraising eye. "You are the younger one, sister to the High Priestess." It was more of a statement than a question. "Where is she?"

"My sister does my father's bidding."

"Meaning that you do not?"

"Meaning nothing of the kind…"

Masters laughed. This young one certainly did not have the presence of the High Priestess, but she was most refreshing.

Leila began to feel slightly uneasy. What had she let herself in for? Well, she had asked for it, and it looked like she was stuck with it.

"Shall we proceed with the tour?"

"Where are you taking me?"

"We will start with a tour of the waterfront and perhaps I can give you a brief history of our nation."

This pleased Masters. He wanted to go to the waterfront to check on The Seeker and, as well, he had been curious from the very beginning to learn more of this world and its people.

Leila led Masters out into the early morning sun. It was still quite cool and the sun was as red as he remembered it. They strolled toward the waterfront and Masters encouraged Leila to talk of Encandor and its people in the hopes of gaining some information that might be of use later on. Despite what the High Priest had said, Masters refused to give up the hope of returning home and intended to continue trying until all avenues were exhausted.

Masters' questions and interest made Leila feel more at ease, and she recounted some of the history of Encandor and her early life in the Temple.

"Our ancestors were once a race of powerful wizards led by the god Balim. There was another race led by another god, Yasha. Yasha became jealous of Balim and sent his warriors, led by Mikael, to destroy Balim and his followers. Mikael was unable to destroy the followers of Balim, who protected his people by hiding them in the nether world and then caused the waters to flow over the sky and, thereby, making them safe from Yasha and his warriors.

"My father, D'Ar, is the successor of a long line of High Priests and has held the position of High Priest of Balim for many dakars. By Temple Law he is permitted to choose his successor. Most assuredly, he will choose Naila, my sister, as his successor for she has found much favor with him, especially of late." She thought of the other day and the sacrifice of her friend.

"I never knew my mother. Her spirit returned to Balim on the day of my birth. By Temple Law my father is refused the right to marry and to have heirs but, so powerful is he, that he took Maora, my mother, a Temple virgin, to wife, and he has elevated my sister Naila, a High Priestess of Balim, to Initiate in the Ancient Mysteries—a position never before held by a woman—and myself he appointed as Keeper of the Flame of Balim.

"My sister was in her First Dakar and I was not yet born when, in the Seventh Dakar of his Oath, by Temple records, D'Ar first made blood sacrifice to Balim and Balim opened the sky and drew D'Ar to his breast in a cloud of fire and smoke. I was born in the Eighth Dakar of D'Ar, and that is when my mother, Maora, returned to Balim."

Masters was taken aback. Blood sacrifice? Now, more than ever, it was imperative to gather all the information possible about this unquestionably sinister place. From just wanting to go home, his feeling had become one of fear and the necessity of escape.

Leila continued, "The people became much in awe of D'Ar, who had been so honored by Balim, and dared not resist him in any manner. The blood sacrifices became more frequent and Balim continued to open the sky and draw D'Ar to him.

"After one such occurrence, the otherworlders appeared on our shores and D'Ar told the people this was a sign from Balim; that, henceforth, Balim himself would provide the sacrificial victims for his altar.

"By this time my sister had begun to show much enthusiasm for the Temple rites and sacrifices, which pleased D'Ar greatly. He began to initiate us both into the rights of the Priesthood of Balim and today my sister rules beside my father.

"At the risk of my father's wrath, for he has forbidden all contact with the otherworlders, after my studies were over for each day and Naila was elsewhere, I would go to a secret place close to the quarters where the otherworlders were held, each awaiting his turn at the altar. These quarters were very well appointed and the otherworlders seemed to want for nothing."

There it was again! Their apparent fate was the altar of this god Balim. He began to see his favored lady in a new light. She apparently was not the dream he had envisioned on his arrival, and the fact that this girl was willing to speak of the sacrifices almost nonchalantly, meant that they truly believed there was no escape.

The narrative continued. "Many hours I would watch and listen and, although they did not speak our language, in other ways they were much like our own people. While the citizens of Encandor are much the same height and complexion, some of the otherworlders were short, some tall, some dark, some light.

"In time, I grew braver and dared approach the otherworlders. At first, the guards were fearful of D'Ar, but I soon won them over, and they allowed me to come and go as I pleased.

"In the years that followed, I began to learn some of the various languages of the otherworlders and was able to communicate. First, of course, to only a small degree, but later on with more success. I found their world to be not too different from ours, but the customs varied widely, and I came at length to the conclusion that the otherworlders were intelligent beings and deserved a somewhat better fate than the Altar of Balim."

She hesitated here as though unsure of her ground. Masters took advantage of this pause. "How is it that a people with such a high technology practices human sacrifice?"

"I know nothing of such things. I know only that, even though a daughter of D'Ar, I wish the practice to cease."

"Is there nothing you can do?"

She hesitated again. Perhaps she had already said too much. Should D'Ar discover, no matter that she was his daughter, she would be severely punished.

"Please, it is also to my benefit, don't you see? From what you have said, there is no future here for us."

A NEW HOPE

He waited as she struggled to make a decision—to trust or not to trust—then, "I found that there were several others who, though fearful of D'Ar, secretly opposed him in the matter of blood sacrifices. I became a member of this secret society, whose aim it was to abolish the sacrifices. It would be a difficult task we knew, for D'Ar enjoyed his position of power and had no intention of relinquishing it easily.

"We struggled in our newly formed society, but never faltered in our search for ways to combat D'Ar. Many persons of note—great scientists, and even some of D'Ar's own advisors—are numbered among us.

"One day, an amazing discovery was made. After the ritual of sacrifice, it was the custom that all but the heart of the victim, which was offered to Balim in a special manner, was put into the furnace and was consumed by the Flame of Balim. By keeping careful watch of all that was done, and the exact time of its doing, we learned that at the moment the flame consumed its victim and Balim drew D'Ar up to him, a phenomenon occurred in the Lake of Kaos. There was a great wind, which would lift up the water and hurl it into the sky, making a fountain of water so high the top disappeared from sight.

"It was while watching one such phenomenon that the real discovery occurred. As the great wind abated and the water settled back into the lake, there was a flash of light that covered the whole sky; and with this light there appeared a strange, small craft, seemingly in midair, which settled down into the water."

"At this particular moment, however, a Temple craft appeared on the horizon speeding toward the strange craft, making further and closer observation imprudent.

"The scientists in our group feel the Flame of Balim has some connection with the phenomenon of the lake and, thereby, the appearance of the otherworlders. It has been noted that, although the phenomenon occurs at each sacrifice, the otherworlders don't always appear at each occurrence. Sometimes it is several weeks, months, years even, between appearances.

"From the scientists who belonged to our society we also learned that D'Ar and his followers had made several attempts to traverse the fountain of water into the sky and into the otherworld—your world. It is not known if any succeeded; those who failed were either blinded by the Eye of Balim or suffered the most horrible of deaths. Of late the attempts have ceased but it is felt that D'Ar will try again. Your world, from what the scientists have told us, is rich in minerals and your technology is advancing rapidly and D'Ar would give much to rule such a world."

By this time, they had reached the pier and Masters could see The Seeker at the far end. He automatically started toward it. Leila, however, held back.

"What is wrong? That's our boat. I want to check it out."

Still she held back. Just then, the door of a nearby building opened and two soldiers walked out and moved toward The Seeker.

Leila grasped his arm. "Please. They must not see me. They would tell my father."

Masters realized the girl was really frightened, so he turned with her in another direction. For the rest of the day, Leila showed him the various sights of Encandor and answered his questions about her people and their customs.

He learned that the Day of Sacrifice was held on the seventh day of each Encandorian "monthly" period, or every twenty-four days. Masters had also noticed that the days were approximately four hours shorter here.

He learned, too, that although it might appear they were prisoners, they were not. Mainly, he supposed, due to the fact that there was no place to go. They were on an island in the middle of a very large lake and there was no boat, other than their own, that they could use in which to flee. And, even if he could get to the boat—and across the lake—according to Leila, most of the inhabitants of the mainland were cannibalistic savages. The people of Encandor never went to the mainland, which she called Mayran, other than soldiers who sometimes brought back some of the gentler natives, who were trained to work in the Temple and the Palace of Iltarn, the nominal ruler of Encandor.

He also questioned her about the Senator, of whom he had heard nothing since their arrival. She promised to inquire and inform Masters of his condition.

He asked her, too, if he would be able to go on board The Seeker and was informed that he could do so, but only with an escort of soldiers. That would not be too helpful, he thought, particularly if Davis were still aboard. He decided not to mention Davis to Leila, even though she had confided in him; perhaps later … when he got to know her better. He felt that for the present, it was best to bide his time.

When they at last returned to the Temple, he reminded her of her promise to check on the Senator, and told her he would look forward to seeing her again. She seemed genuinely pleased at the prospect.

*   *   *

Davis was glad that yesterday was over. Strange people had come to gawk and some had even boarded the yacht for a look around. He was in his cabin, having just awakened, when he heard the first one come on board. He thought then that it was the crew coming back, and he had rushed out in the passageway just in time to see a young woman in a long, pale green robe peer around the corner. He had stepped back into the doorway quickly, but not quite before she had seen him and he heard her scream.

Then he heard the soldiers come on board, and an argument ensued. But the soldiers finally put everyone off the boat and, as it appeared they were going to search the boat again, he quickly went to the engine room to his own personal hiding place. He was in such a hurry to hide, he had forgotten to take his bottle and, while in actuality it was only about half an hour, the inspection seemed to take several hours.

It was now midday and Davis had been lying on deck for the better part of an hour. He had his binoculars and had been checking the inspection schedule so that tonight, perhaps, he could slip off the yacht and check out the area around the waterfront. He still was concerned about the crew and passengers. Though he had convinced himself they were still alive—his only sanity in this insanity—he could not understand why at least someone had not returned to the boat. There was a chance, however slight, that he could locate the crew or Perrin or even Charley and learn what had happened to them. Maybe they were prisoners—or worse.

Oh, no, he thought. Here come some more "tourists." It appeared to be a man and a woman. He adjusted the focus on his glasses to get a better look. The two were strolling nonchalantly down the pier, the girl talking and the man listening. As they approached, Davis thought there was something familiar about the man. He waited until they were a few yards closer and adjusted the focus again. Could it be…? Yes, it was Masters.

He started to rise from his position of concealment, when the door of the warehouse opened and two soldiers came out. He saw the girl grasp Masters' arm and turn him away. "NO!" He tightened his grip on the glasses and gritted his teeth. "No, you must not leave. Don't leave me here alone." But Masters WAS leaving and the soldiers were coming toward the yacht for another of their inspections. Now, more than ever, he must go ashore. He MUST find the crew! And Masters. Or, maybe he could find Perrin. Anyone!

Though his subconscious mind now knew that the crew and passengers were alive, his conscious mind could think of nothing other than the fact that he was being deserted once again. He reached out in supplication, rubbing the magic lamp of his mind WILLING Masters to return—NOW.

How long he was in this posture, he could not tell, but the soldiers were getting closer and now he must get below to avoid detection. Tonight! Yes, tonight he would do a little reconnaissance. Right now, though, he felt a sudden thirst. A drink! Yes, that's what he needed. A drink to calm his shattered nerves. Thank God the soldiers had not removed the supplies. He slipped down the ladder toward his cabin.

*   *   *

Leila admired her mirrored image as her servant put the finishing touches to her hairdo. She had just completed dressing for an informal audience with Iltarn.

Things were not going as planned. She had somehow managed to get through the balance of the tour with Masters the other day, but the incident on the waterfront had unsettled her. One of the soldiers had looked their way and she was sure that he had recognized her. It seemed to her that it was only a matter of time before the word got back to D'Ar.

And now—NOW, things were getting worse. Iltarn, the Emperor, had called for an informal review of the strangers. She had wondered why, since he had taken no particular interest in any of the prior occurrences. It irritated her because now she would have to put off contacting Masters for yet another while. No, things were not running smoothly at all.

The informal review was to be held via closed-circuit hookup between the Temple and the Palace. Iltarn rarely left the Palace. In fact, her only memory of his leaving the Palace was in the stories told her as a child by some of her father's ministers.

Many times, however, she had pictured him in her mind. Of course, she had seen likenesses of him in public places—he was tall; taller even than her father. She thought of him as ancient. No one seemed really to know how long Iltarn had been Emperor of Encandor. Even the historical books she had read in her schooling made no mention of a predecessor.

And, the stories she had heard made him seem so evil and decadent she was sure, should she ever see him in the flesh, that he would be the ugliest and foulest of beings. The very thought of even an informal review was repulsive to her, notwithstanding the fact that she would not see him nor would he see her.

D'Ar, Naila, and Leila were situated in the main observation chamber where D'Ar could direct the proceedings first hand. A technician was punching out a code on the control panel. A picture flashed on the screen. It showed an empty room. More buttons were pressed at a wave of D'Ar's hand. A new scene flashed into view. Leila recognized the black man in the group. D'Ar impatiently waved this picture away as well. A third scene showed the women's quarters. There were three women seated in the lounging room, quietly conversing. This was the first time Leila had gotten a really close look at the women. The camera centered on a tall, dark-haired woman of about forty. The technician looked for approval, but D'Ar shook his head. The camera then focused on another dark-haired woman with finely chiseled features. D'Ar again shook his head.

The third woman in the room had risen from her chair and was now impatiently pacing about the room. She was obviously irritated and was becoming very animated in her speech and gestures. She stopped for a moment and the camera focused on her face.

"Ah, yes!" Leila's attention was momentarily drawn from the screen as she turned to seek out the speaker. The remark was repeated and Leila realized that the words were not spoken by anyone in the room. It must have been Iltarn.

She quickly glanced at the screen. The girl pictured there had a tiny frown on her face. Her action seemed suspended, as though she, too, had heard the remark. She was a lovely girl with short, blond hair and a definite air of independence.

Leila looked at her father, who seemed very pleased with himself. "Father, what does this mean?"

"Mean?" He smiled. "My child, it means Encandor."

That evening, while D'Ar was away from the Temple on business, Naila eagerly explained all the implications of the afternoon's incident. Long had there been enmity between their father and Iltarn and D'Ar sought to placate the Emperor through his own belief of the lascivious nature of the Emperor, thus his intention of making a gift of this girl to Iltarn.

Leila could hardly believe her ears. "But, why?"

"To insure non-interference from the Palace, of course. How do you think Father has managed all these years, anyway?"

With this final remark, Naila drew herself up to her full height, lifted her lovely chin, and walked ceremoniously from the room.

*   *   *

Jennifer was angry and irritated. From the beginning, they were separated from the rest of the party; and poor Helen, how was she to manage without Sim? This was the first time they had been separated since they had been married.

That PRIEST had made promises and then proceeded to break them. He had said they would be able to move about and take a tour of the city. In actuality, they had been LOCKED in these tiny quarters since the audience. Their meals had even been delivered to them here—it was a wonder that the three of them had been permitted to stay together. Talk about the Middle Ages; these were the DARK AGES. She somehow felt that they had been thrown back in time and only the technology she had seen had given the lie to that.

She, Helen and Tiffany had been conversing quietly about their sad situation when Tiffany told them she felt as though she had been watched from a hidden place on the day of their arrival. Jen now stood and started to pace the room. Suddenly, the hair at the back of her neck prickled. Stopping dead in her tracks, she frowned and looked at Tiffany questioningly. Tiffany's nod was almost imperceptible.

As quickly as it had come, the feeling was gone but Jen was very uncomfortable. She tried to shrug it off without success and excused herself to avoid making the others as uncomfortable as she. There was a definite sense of foreboding in the air.

*   *   *

Nikto watched Naila as the technician manipulated the buttons on the panel. He thought he detected a faint glimmer of interest when the camera flashed on his tall, dark beauty but he could not be sure. The camera moved on to the shorter blond stranger and he heard Iltarn's approval, after which all had departed.

Now, he was back in the chamber as he had been each day since that first experience; he was fascinated with this dark-haired stranger. Whenever duty permitted, he would be here, as he was now. His fingers played over the panel; everything was set, he had merely to press the final button, but he was somehow hesitant, fearful that she might be gone.

With grim determination, he pressed the button and the room leapt into view. Tiffany (he marvelled at the beauty of her name—he had taken many pains to learn it without being found out) was lying in a relaxed position on a lounge chair. Her head was thrown back and her eyes were closed. Suddenly, she jumped up and ran from the room. Nikto hurriedly reset the buttons and the scene changed to the common room of the women's quarters. There he saw a soldier standing at the door, while another was busily going from room to room, obviously searching for someone. He finally emerged from one of the rooms with the blond girl in tow. She was struggling, but he kept a firm grip on her arm.

Tiffany started toward the struggling pair, but was caught up from behind by a third soldier, who apparently was just out of view of the camera. He held her until the other two had removed the young girl from the quarters.

71

The third woman was standing statue-still in a doorway with her hand covering her mouth, obviously in a state of shock.

After the last soldier had finally left the room, Tiffany took the other woman by the hand and led her into the bedroom. Nikto shut off the camera. There would be no more pleasure in watching any more of this scene and he had been away from his duties long enough this day.

*   *   *

"Leila, what are you doing here?"

Leila's heart quickened as she heard Naila's voice.

"I wanted to see the old one."

"For what purpose?"

Leila was always at a disadvantage where Naila was concerned. And, now, she felt as though she had been caught sneaking a sweetmeat or peeking at a present before the proper time. Besides, Naila knew perfectly well that Leila had every right to be here—didn't she help in the clinic from time to time?

"I have never seen one so advanced in time. Even our father is not so ancient—only Iltarn."

Naila smiled maliciously. "And?"

"His spirit has returned to Balim." Leila was visibly saddened.

"It is not well that you have anything to do with the otherworlders. You know it is forbidden by D'Ar."

"What about you?"

"WHAT ABOUT ME?" Naila's manner turned icy.

Leila had felt the injustice of Naila's power before and was in no mood to test her sister's patience or her good will. "Please forgive me, Naila. I spoke too hastily. It was only the disappointment of not being able to see the old one."

Though only slightly taller than Leila, Naila now seemed a full head taller as she looked into Leila's eyes, her own flashing triumphantly. Without further word, she turned and walked away.

*   *   *

The next several days were filled with tours and indoctrination classes. Masters and, he assumed, the others had learned more of the history of Encandor. From his vast experience and studies over the years, it seemed to him that these people ran a remarkable parallel to the ancient Mayan civilization. Who's to say the Mayans did not have an advanced technology at one time or another in their past?

He learned, too, more about the people themselves. It seemed that they either worked on the farms growing food, in the Temple in the service of D'Ar, or in the palace in the service of Iltarn. Not too much variety to choose from and absolutely NO free enterprise.

There were no animals on Encandor. He had seen sculptures of some animals from home and portraits of others, but when he questioned his guide, he was told only that there were no animals.

Other than fresh vegetables, cotton (or something like it) for clothing, and fruit-bearing vines (he saw nothing that even closely resembled a tree), everything was manufactured, though Masters had not actually seen the process.

Their arts were surprising for so limited a culture. Their sculptures, paintings and other fine arts rivaled his own world's old masters. He had not yet visited one of their museums of "living art" nor had he attended any of their musical offerings and was looking forward to these with anticipation and interest. He could have enjoyed himself so much more, as on upper earth (he could not keep himself from calling this world "inner earth" though it did have sun and sky), had he not the worry of his future and that of his companions.

He did attend a unique sports event unlike anything he had ever seen. It was played with six people—three on either team—with a ball that, for want of a better description, was "alive." It seemed to have a mind of its own. The object of the game

73

apparently was to capture the ball and hold it for several seconds, thereby gaining points for one's side. Not only did one have to contend with the opponent, the ball had its own ideas. At one juncture, it appeared deliberately to tap one player on the shoulder and by the time the player had turned, the ball was off in another direction. All the players, as well as the spectators, seemed to be having a wonderful time. It would be something to take home, if indeed any of them ever got home.

He also was permitted to visit an observatory. Encandor had no stars as such, nor did it have a moon. Just the sun, which was visible for ten hours each day, leaving the world in darkness for about six. He learned that it never varied. At night, there was only artificial light from a source which was not unlike that on the spacecraft. At least he thought it to be artificial. It could very well come from a natural source, such as bacteria.

Were it not for D'Ar's power, Encandor presented an almost idealistic communal society. Of course, he had not yet been permitted to visit any of the various workers in their home atmosphere. That might present an entirely different picture. From what he could see, however, these people were well adapted to their isolated island life, contributing their talents to, and receiving their needs from, the community. He wondered that he had not yet seen anyone who appeared to be under the age of eighteen or so. This was a question he had put to one of his guides but was met with a flat refusal to discuss the matter and one thing conspicuously absent was any mention of the religion of Encandor or of sacrifices of any kind. Masters, likewise, made no mention to any of the others of his discussion with Leila. Perhaps it was best that they did not know what fate awaited them. If, indeed, that fate did await them.

He was beginning, too, to understand some of the terms of Encandor and had even picked up some of the language. For instance, he learned that a dakar was loosely translated into about seven years of his time. His watch showed him they had been here four days—upper earth time—though this was the morning of the fifth day here.

Interspersed among the tours were sessions with personnel from the Temple. These were spent in acquainting their hosts with more of the customs and mores of the world left behind. Masters felt no reason to hold back information since it would be forthcoming from the rest of the cruise members, and he did not wish to arouse any suspicions in the Encandorians which would limit his own gathering of knowledge.

Thinking now reminded him of their plight and the fact that he had not seen Leila since the day of the first tour. In fact, he had not even seen Nikto. And, although they kept the days full, he was getting a little anxious about what had happened to the Senator.

His thoughts drifted back and forth between Leila and Naila and the differences between them. Perhaps Leila had told him the story because of jealousy of her sister, but she had seemed so sincere. Well, it certainly seemed that she had forgotten him quickly enough after the tour was over. He tried, but still could not dismiss her from his mind.

Maybe he would see her again tomorrow: At the end of the last class today, it had been announced that the group would be presented to Iltarn the next morning.

He had just lain back on his pillow when he heard a whisper.

"Masters!" He sat up and looked around.

"Be not alarmed." It was Leila's voice, but she was nowhere to be seen.

"Where…?" He started.

"Quiet. I wish not to be discovered. Stroll out into the corridor. I will meet you."

Masters rose from his bed, checked to see if Perrin was awake—he was not—then went out into the corridor.

Leila waited just beyond the door. "If my sister knew I was here, there would be much trouble. I think she suspects something is amiss. Perhaps when I questioned the nurse about your friend."

"How is he?" Masters asked anxiously.

"His spirit returned to Balim two days hence. I have just now been able to come to you, I have been watched so closely."

Then the Senator was dead. Masters felt a pang of sorrow. Perhaps, though, it was for the best, all things considered.

Leila left him alone with his thoughts for a moment, then "Tomorrow you are to be taken before Iltarn."

"Yes, we were told."

"But, what you have not been told, is that the one called Jennifer is to be made a gift to Iltarn by my father, D'Ar."

"Jennifer? Given to Iltarn? Is there nothing we can do to stop this?"

"I am working on a plan to get you and the others away; however, it must wait until after the Presentation tomorrow. I fear I cannot help your friend. Perhaps, later, we can find a way to free her. But all of you must go to the Presentation, otherwise any plan would be doomed to failure before it began. Please trust me."

She took his hands in hers and looked up into his eyes. He could see sorrow, hope, determination. "Of course I trust you." Masters said the words with much hope. He did trust her, but to what avail. What could one small girl do against the world of Encandor.

He watched as she moved off down the corridor and out of sight, then returned to his room and another sleepless night.

PHILADELPHIA FREEDOM NEWS
Philadelphia, Pa. December 11, …
SEARCH FOR "THE SEEKER" ABANDONED
All Aboard Presumed Lost

API, Miami, Florida

Coast Guard sources stated today that, after five days, it was abandoning the search, in which it was joined by the Navy and several private pilots, for The Seeker, a 110-foot yacht belonging to millionaire philanthropist Alex Perrin. The search covered an area of approximately 10,000 sq. miles; however, no sign of survivors or wreckage was found.

The search commenced on December 6, after a distress call was received in the early morning. As nearly as could be determined from the garbled message, The Seeker apparently was encountering gale force winds and its position was about midway between Puerto Rico, its last port of call, and Bermuda, its ultimate destination. Informed sources have reported that The Seeker left the port of San Juan on December 1.

Listed among the missing are owner Alex Perrin; Senator Wayne Danton (D.Tex); his Administrative Assistant Donald Martin; multimillionaire playboy Reginald C. Masters, III; J. Simpson Barron, Chief Executive Officer of Lasko Oil Company, and his wife Helen; Jennifer Barron Craig, Fashion Editor of Today's World; Tiffany Crist, model and cover girl; and a crew of seven.

JENNIFER'S PLIGHT

She had never considered herself a stubborn person—really, she was not; however, Jen decided it was time to take a definitive stand. She had been DRAGGED from her room and put into a harem—there was no other word for it. Except … all the girls kept here were considerably younger than she. The youngest could easily be eight or nine and the eldest was about twenty or twenty-one. To be sure, there were some matronly types but these appeared to be workers who took care of the girls and taught them protocol and decorum. They were now trying to teach her, for what purpose she could not imagine.

They had pleaded and cajoled but she was determined that she would NOT give in. Whatever purpose they had in mind, she intended to know more before complying with their wishes. What did she care that these women were under orders from someone else?

It had seemed like such a lark when they had arrived in this new world—exciting even. Now it was becoming a bore and she was more than a little frightened.

"I am told you are resisting."

A new voice, though not unfriendly.

Jen turned to look into the kindest eyes she had seen since their arrival.

"I am Delia. What is your name?"

"Jennifer … Jen to my friends."

"Jennifer … Jen, I'd like to be your friend."

Jen was caught completely off-guard. This woman was obviously not one of the "hired help." She was dressed in a pale yellow caftan with traces of aqua running through the weave. Gold metallic slippers peaked from beneath the edges of her hem. Jen estimated that she was about forty years of age. She had gentle brown eyes and soft, curly brown hair, which she wore shoulder length.

She put her hand on Jen's shoulder. "Come," she said, "let's get to know each other."

Jen allowed herself to be led to a small room containing some overstuffed chairs and fabric-covered benches. She was completely at ease with this woman.

Delia acquainted her with some of the customs of the Temple and of the people of Encandor. She learned that the girls were not actually part of a harem, but were being trained in the service of the Temple and some were to be honored as the Bride of Balim from time to time but Delia would not expound on this further. She also was told that Delia, although a scientist, was in the service of the Temple and had the ultimate responsibility of the training of those in the service of the Temple, such as these girls.

Too, she was in charge of the nursery, which was a communal affair where ALL the children were kept after weaning until age four. From age four to age eight, the children were schooled in all the arts, the sciences, history, language, etc. At age eight, it was then decided by a committee where each child's talents could best be used, whether farming, domestics, Temple or palace service, etc. These children, then, were trained to serve in that particular field until age sixteen, at which time they entered service.

Alliances were formed in two steps: With the exception of those girls chosen to serve Balim, from age fourteen both boys and girls attended various functions held at the Temple, the palace and the pavilion (a place not connected with either the Temple or the palace) on a stag basis. There was absolutely NO pairing. At age eighteen, there was "permitted pairings" but with one requirement—there could be no less than three and no more than five possible combinations of pairs for each boy or girl. From these separate pairings, another committee then made what it considered a suitable match for either boy or girl, thus permitting each boy or girl a choice, but not the ultimate decision. Alliances were for life. There was no exception.

With regard to the girls in the service of Balim, if they were not chosen to be the Bride of Balim by age twenty-two, these girls were permitted another field of their own choice. If they wished an alliance, a choice of suitable mates was provided, the opposite of the accepted method of alliance.

Jen was appalled but, the more she thought on it, realized that her own life was a prime example of "freedom of choice." Not a very pretty picture either way.

When Jen was quite at ease, Delia informed her of her own particular fate in a couple of days. Her mind rebelled at the very thought but she did, at Delia's request, allow the serving women to prepare her for the presentation to Iltarn. Imagining that this could ever come to pass in the twentieth century was beyond her immediate comprehension.

*   *   *

Masters and the others were awakened early. The slaves who had attended them since their arrival brought in special clothing for the Presentation. Special in that, instead of the usual green, they were of a mauve color with a gold band. At least this is what the men were given. They had not been permitted to see the women since the initial audience with D'Ar. He had wondered about this and questioned one of the servants who had a smattering of English. All that he was able to learn was that they were all right, which was no small comfort in view of what he had learned from Leila.

The Temple was abuzz with excitement. It seemed that very few strangers were presented to Iltarn, and Masters wondered what made this group so special. Then he remembered what Leila had said about Jennifer. But, what made her so special? Tiffany was equally as beautiful.

The men were ushered into a special aircar for their trip to the Palace, which was some distance away. Masters speculated on the reason why the Palace was so far away as everything else

80

was within walking distance of the Temple. He wondered if it was by imperial decree or by D'Ar's decree.

The caravan passed through a small park with sculptures both modern and renaissance in design. There was a small gazebo on one side of the pathway and on the other was a flower garden. He was glad to see that someone at least took pride in the beauty of nature.

Strangely, however, there was no one in the park at all. He must ask about this. Perhaps there was no one in Encandor who worked at night and was at ease during the day. But, surely, there should be SOMEONE in the park, even if it were just on their way to their jobs.

All in all, it took about thirty minutes of travelling time and gave Masters a chance to view a little more of Encandor. He noted that there were few people on the streets. New York was never like this at 9:00 a.m. He made a mental note to question his next guide on the population of Encandor. He already knew something of their likes and dislikes—they were not unlike his own. But as to how many, he had just never thought to ask before.

The outside of the Palace was much like the other buildings of Encandor—a block style at the bottom, which might continue upward for several levels, or might be graduated to smaller floors and, finally, much like a spire or pinnacle, but in a larger fashion. The interior, however, put the Temple to shame. Every manner of luxury was apparent. Lush velvets, rich failles, transparent silks. All were in evidence as well as brocades and furs. Furs! Where did they come from? Perhaps they were not real, but they certainly looked real, especially the leopard and tiger. He had already learned there were no animals here. Another question for Leila when he saw her again.

They were ushered into a sort of waiting room just outside the Presentation Hall. There were padded benches with short backs, lined up as pews in a church, and one wall was covered with heavy crimson drapes. Masters took a peek behind the draperies and, through a plate glass window, looked down upon a great hall with similar benches lining either side and a crimson runner stretching from massive double doors at one end to the opposite wall. This wall was draped with fine, multi-colored silks. He squinted his eyes, the better to peer through the transparent hangings, but was unable to see anything, as though the drapes merely covered a wall, but to what purpose? There must be something back there, but he simply could not make it out.

Exactly opposite was another window with similar draperies, also closed. The lower edge of the window was about three feet above the floor of the hall, and he presumed the window from which he was peering was the same. He wondered if the women might be behind those curtains.

Groups of people, dressed in various styles and bright colors, were coming in from small side entrances and seating themselves on the benches.

At this time the soldier who escorted them from the Temple opened the door and asked that they be seated on the benches. It was but a moment later that the curtains opened before them. He now could look directly across the hall to the other window. He was disappointed to see only D'Ar, Naila and Leila. Tiffany, Jennifer and Helen were nowhere to be seen.

His eye caught a movement at the wall containing the drapes, and he turned just in time to see two men, dressed in red uniforms, not unlike Nikto's uniform, step from behind the silks. Each had a long trumpet which he raised to his lips and blew. He was surprised, as he had expected a blast, but instead he heard a clear, sweet melody he had not thought possible from such a horn. When the music ended, the curtains parted to reveal a figure dressed in white satin and seated on a large, golden throne. For a crown, he had a simple gold band around his forehead. In the center of the band was a gold coin with no markings, and extending upwards were two thin circles of color, one red and one green. There was no question about it. This was Iltarn.

Iltarn was a little hard to figure out. He looked quite dapper in his satin suit, which appeared to be eighteenth century European, but his face belied this. He had the lean, hungry look of a hawk. From what Leila had told him, Iltarn was nothing more than a figurehead. The rest of her description certainly did not fit. Neither was he "ancient" nor did he seem repulsive. Rather, he appeared to be the same age as the High Priest and this made Masters wonder what could have happened to force him into this kind of role. More questions to be asked—if he lived long enough.

While Masters was speculating on Iltarn, some of the people were being presented to him, probably with requests or problems of some sort. Some took only a short time, while others took longer. Masters figured that they had been in the observation room waiting for probably an hour before the final petitioner had come forth.

The trumpets sounded again and all eyes in the hall turned toward the massive doors. Masters turned also, just in time to see them swing quietly inward and D'Ar enter. He had been so engrossed in his own thoughts, he had not even seen D'Ar leave the booth. He was now striding toward the throne. Behind him followed Nikto, directly ahead of two soldiers. Between the two soldiers was a squirming Jennifer, struggling to free herself from her captors. There was a gasp from the hall as she finally broke loose from their grasp, took a little running step to get in front of them. She turned with a look of utter disdain, then stiffened her back, held her head high, and proceeded toward the throne. Her floor-length gown, of the flimsiest gauze gathered at neck, wrist, and waist, was iridescent and shimmered in the morning light with each determined step she took. The soldiers looked somewhat bewildered, but made no move to restrain her again.

Upon seeing Jennifer in her struggle to free herself from her captors, Masters and Perrin immediately, involuntarily, rose to go to her aid. Still in the process of turning to leave the booth, Masters felt a hand on his shoulder, then a sharp pain so intense it clouded his mind for an instant and he literally slumped back into his chair. From the corner of his eye, he saw Perrin also drop back into his chair. This was something new to him but most effective since it had immobilized two strong men in a single instant. He made a mental note to ask Nikto about the procedure. Even now, he had to massage the muscle to relieve some of the stress.

By this time, D'Ar had reached the foot of the throne. He bowed low and, with a sweeping gesture, pointed to Jennifer. "Iltarn, Ruler of Encandor, Mighty Conqueror of Mayran, Son of Soldar, and Leader of the Faithful of Balim, I, D'Ar, present to you this fair maiden, who is called Jennifer, to grace your house." He motioned to Jennifer to step forward.

Jennifer, however, stood her ground. D'Ar gave a slight start, then apparently changed his mind. "Girl," he said in a low voice, "do not tempt the gods. Accept your fate. Far better than another I could have planned for you." He motioned slightly with his head.

Jennifer apparently had been told or realized the portent of D'Ar's threat and curtsied deeply before Iltarn. "Your grace, it is with great anticipation and pleasure that I come to the House of Iltarn. I am yours to command."

Jennifer could have bitten her tongue. Was it she really saying those words? D'Ar had looked so ominous that she felt this to be the better path for the moment.

Iltarn motioned for her to come forward, appraising her carefully as she moved up the dais to stand beside the throne. Immediately thereafter, the trumpets sounded again, and the curtains closed on the two of them. She was beginning now to question her choice as she saw the look of cunning in Iltarn's eyes.

* * *

Jennifer stood very still for a few seconds after the drapes had closed, then, placing her hands purposefully on her hips, she turned toward Iltarn, eyes flashing angrily. "Just exactly what is the meaning of this? If you think I'm going to…"

Iltarn raised his finger in a gesture of silence. "If you will accompany me, your questions will be answered."

He stood and took her gently by one arm as if to lead her away.

"I can walk by myself."

"As you wish." He started away from her at a brisk walk. She stood for a moment, looking first at the curtain, then at the emperor's retreating back. She instinctively knew it would be hopeless to try to escape, so she turned to follow Iltarn. He was a considerable distance ahead of her by this time and she had to run to catch up. She barely caught up to him as he turned the corner and strode through an open doorway. She just managed to slip through before a uniformed guard closed the door.

"Sir?"

Jennifer was startled as Iltarn whirled around. "Young woman," he began, "I'm sorry to have put you through such torment, but I assure you my intentions are most honorable. Can I depend upon your discretion?"

"I don't understand…"

"I am asking for your trust and, in turn, I am willing to give you mine."

She still looked puzzled, so he hastened to explain further. "Many years ago, before D'Ar, the religion and government of Encandor were intertwined. It was a practical, as well as beneficial, partnership. Then, the spirit of Mesto returned to Balim, leaving D'Ar as the logical choice for High Priest.

"D'Ar had been tutored by Mesto and it appeared that the partnership would continue as before. The status quo remained for a time, but it soon became apparent that D'Ar was more ambitious than his predecessor and wished complete rule of Encandor.

"How long his plans had been in the offing is not known; however, it is presumed that he had been working on his ultimate takeover even prior to the demise of Mesto. It is not even beyond belief that he had a hand in the untimely death of Mesto, although there is no evidence of such."

"Why didn't you just stop him? You were ruler of Encandor, weren't you?"

He smiled. Youth seemed always to know the answers. What could they not teach their elders given half a chance.

"That is exactly my plan; however, I would prefer it to be without a civil war. Some of the soldiers in my employ are loyal to D'Ar. Likewise, some of the soldiers in his employ are loyal to me. It would be a bloody war, one for which I have no taste. No, it must be done with intrigue and finesse."

"How might I be of help? I am most certainly—was most certainly a prisoner and my position here does not seem to be much better."

"I accepted D'Ar's gift as a means only. In this way, I could at least save one from his bloody sacrifices. You are free to go if you wish."

"But, where would I go?"

"Precisely why I am soliciting your aid. If we are successful, you will be free to go wherever you wish."

"Will I be able to go home?"

"That, I am afraid, is beyond my power. You would have it if I could give it."

"Very well, I am willing to listen to your plan."

A PLAN

December 15, …

It was several days now that Jen had been with Iltarn and he still had not revealed his plan to her. She only knew that he was kind, considerate and actually, quite nice. Still smarting somewhat from her recent divorce, Jen was truly grateful for his kindness. She was, however, concerned about her friends. She had been given a handmaiden by the name of Seriha to help her with various small duties and they had become quite close. Seriha counted herself fortunate to be in the service of the Emperor rather than to be Virgin of Balim; it was always better to live. She had explained to Jen the rules of Encandor as well as the dangers of remaining in the Temple at the mercy of D'Ar and Naila.

It was Seriha who told Jen that Tiffany was slated for the Altar of Balim at the next Ritual Sacrifice in the not too distant future. Jen had cried for two days and nights. Finally, she decided to implore Iltarn to interfere on behalf of her friend. He was reluctant to do so for fear that it would interfere with his over-all plans to change Encandor but he had come to adore this sweet, sweet otherworlder and could not see her so unhappy. He did have a plan, just formulated, but it would require her cooperation.

"Anything"!

"Do not so readily agree. You may find what I have planned to be distasteful, though necessary."

With tear-filled eyes, Jen said once again "Anything. I will do anything you say. I trust you with all my heart."

Yet she was quite taken aback at his next statement. "I would make Alliance with you. Alliance is a binding of two people together forever."

She swallowed quickly, then with a brave new face, and as she wiped the last tears from her eyes, she quickly appraised the situation. She had become really fond of Iltarn and, as there was truly no hope of returning home, she said with finality "I accept your proposal."

He outlined his plans, indicating that she could have her two friends in the ceremony, after which he would have them secreted away. She immediately agreed, and they moved quickly to put everything in motion.

With Seriha's help, Jen planned for the wedding. First, the gown. It must be white satin, trimmed in gold. They finally chose a strapless gown with a straight neckline, fitted to the hips and gently flared from there to the floor. There was a cuff across the top made of gold satin. Her headdress would be in the shape of a miter, also of white satin and trimmed with gold binding. Her slippers were high-heeled slides with a single gold rose on the toe of each one. Now that the wedding dress, etc. was decided upon, they continued planning for the ceremony. D'Ar would, of course, perform the ceremony; that was a necessity. He MUST be a participant. She would have four attendants, her two friends from home and two of the ladies of the palace. She would have chosen Seriha if it were permitted, but she being a servant, it was not. Her attendants would likewise wear gowns of satin, but would be pink with red trim. Now it was time to plan the reception. They decided the reception would be an intimate affair, a sit-down dinner, and the favors would be small individual cakes for each person in attendance, together with one glass of milset (Jennifer found this to be the libation closest in appearance and taste to champagne that she could find).

*   *   *

Naila read the announcement with dismay. Another irritation in her life which she did not need at this time. Iltarn had decided to make Jennifer his Empress. And, he intended to allow the two otherworlder women to be in the ceremony. All of this was entirely unheard of; however, she dared not approach her father on this matter. Too many times in the past had she

88

complained to him and to even speak of this with him would be to no avail. While D'Ar's powers greatly exceeded those of the Emperor, Naila was sure that he would do absolutely nothing to interfere with this new development. She looked again at the announcement.

ILTARN
Emperor of Encandor

is pleased and privileged to announce that

on the Twentieth Day of Metrino in the year 24789.12

Ms. Jennifer Craig

will join in Alliance with

ILTARN

and be elevated in status to

Empress of Encandor

*   *   *

AND, to top it all off, there was a second card commanding the presence of D'Ar and his daughters. This was an impossible situation. To think that Iltarn would even entertain, much less make it a "command performance," of elevating an otherworlder to such a position. Of course, there had been no other occasion in all her years in which there had even been a small possibility of an otherworlder to come to a position of power.

She finally did mention her feelings to D'Ar but, as she expected, he refused to do anything about it, or even try. He told her he was to officiate and did he not make a gift of the girl to Iltarn? This did not please her but, as she had few days to prepare, the Alliance being set only four days hence, she set her mind to work on details. She must have a special gown; it would never do to be outdone by an offworlder. And she was off to prepare.

*   *   *

The great day finally arrived. This was quite a different situation than when Masters and his friends were in the Palace of the Emperor. They had not been told of the occasion of this new visit and neither Nikto nor Leila had any idea other than it was at the command of the Emperor. He, Sim, Alex and Donald sat together in a box-like structure similar to a box in a theater. To their immediate left was another box, this containing D'Ar, Naila and Leila. Try as he might, he could not get Leila's eye, even though the boxes were at a slight angle. He could barely see that there was another box on the other side of the one containing D'Ar and his daughters, but was unable to see who was in it.

He wondered if the crew were also to attend. While they were in the same quarters, they were extended different privileges.

Below and in front of the boxes were several benches upon which, apparently, were all the inhabitants of Encandor. In all his time here, he had never seen so many people, and all gathered in one place, too. He wondered if they knew what was going on.

His speculations were interrupted by the arrival of the two trumpeters as before. This time, however, the fanfare was more pronounced and of a greater length. At the end of it, the curtains directly facing the three boxes opened and D'Ar stepped through. Now, when did he leave the box and Masters wondered where his mind was that he did not notice. There was a flurry of excitement and applause which made Masters believe that they, at least, knew what to expect. Again, the music, and two women stepped through, dressed in identical gowns of pink satin with red trim. These women were complete strangers to him and he assumed they were of the palace. Following these two came two more, dressed identically to the first two. He was truly shocked to recognize Tiffany and Helen. What were they doing here? Before he could speculate further, another woman entered, dressed in white satin accented with gold. She wore a white satin headdress much in the shape of a miter, also trimmed with gold. She wore a veil covering every part of her face, except her eyes. He put his hands across his brow to shade his eyes from the glare of the lights shining down from the ceiling in an effort to identify the woman. It was impossible. Following the woman was Iltarn; there was no mistaking him. That was one face he would never forget even though he had seen it only once; he had taken Jen and that was something else he would never forget. After all, Jen was his friend, even if their acquaintance had covered only a very short period of time. And Masters was always true to his friends.

D'Ar had begun to speak: "Citizens of Encandor and honored guests from the otherworld, it is with great pleasure and honor that I bind this man and this woman in Alliance." With that he faced the man and woman and, using a gold and silver chain, he bound Iltarn's left hand to the right hand of the woman. That done, he removed the woman's veil. Masters was so surprised that he heard none of the balance of the ceremony. It was Jen. Now, why on earth would she marry this Iltarn? Did she no longer desire to return home? He wished he could talk with her for just a moment. He wanted to know if she really, really knew what she was doing to her life by tying herself to this man, regardless of the fact that he was the Emperor of this land.

He regained his senses barely in time to see the two embrace and kiss. Just the short period he had known Jen, he knew her to be sensible and not given to rash judgment; and he felt he must accept her judgment and her reasoning for whatever plan she might have in mind and for whatever reason she might have.

He snapped out of his reverie in time to see the couple start down the aisle, smiling and waving to the guests. He looked closely into the face of Jen as she walked toward him; she looked up to the box with a radiant smile on her face and waved to her friends. She certainly did look happy.

Just then, a palace servant entered the box and indicated that the men should accompany him to the reception. Maybe he would get a chance to speak with Jen there. This was not to be. She and Iltarn were completely surrounded by various citizens of Encandor, together with Naila and D'Ar.

He was still looking for an opportunity when he felt a tug on his sleeve and looked down. It was Leila. She smile, blew him a kiss, then rushed off to join her father and her sister. The secretiveness and mystery gave Masters a little thrill and he smiled to himself. What a pixie she was.

After she was gone, he looked for Helen and Tiffany but they were nowhere in sight. He checked with Sim, who most certainly would have been watching, and was told that the two women were taken by Temple guards immediately after the ceremony, supposedly back to the Temple.

After the reception was over, Jen asked Iltarn about her friends. He told her the bad news. D'Ar apparently had taken precautions against the very action they had planned and had them taken away right after the ceremony; however, he said there would be another opportunity soon and he surely would save her friends.

ON BOARD THE SEEKER

December 17, …

More waiting. It had been two days since the Alliance of Jen and Iltarn; long, dreary days and Masters had not yet heard from Leila. He dared not speak to the others of any plans, for fear of raising false hopes. Feeling very despondent, he had asked for a tour of the waterfront, and was now on his way together with Charley whom he had asked to go along in the slim hope that, should they be lucky enough to board The Seeker, he might slip away and determine what had become of the captain. A pleasant young man by the name of Antius was their guide.

As they reached the slip where The Seeker was tied, the two soldiers assigned to inspect the craft periodically had just completed their rounds, and Antius had little trouble in persuading them that it was unnecessary that they accompany his tour through the boat.

When Antius explained that he had never before seen a primitive craft such as The Seeker, and exhibited curiosity as to the mechanics of running it, Masters was all too anxious to show him throughout the entire craft, explaining in minute detail the workings of the engines, etc., giving Charley a perfect opportunity to slip away.

Almost immediately, however, Antius noticed his absence and would have instituted a search had not Masters explained that Charley merely had gone to another part of the boat so that he, Masters, could demonstrate the communications system within the craft. He picked up a mike and pressed the transmission button. "Charley, please come in."

Only an instant later, "Yes sir, Mr. Reginald."

"Where are you now?"

"I am in the galley, sir."

"Charley, when you have completed checking the galley, please meet us in the wheelhouse."

"Yes sir, Mr. Reginald."

Antius was delighted by this demonstration, satisfied that nothing was amiss, and they continued on through the passengers' quarters and up onto the deck. There Masters suggested that they await Charley as he did not wish the soldiers to note that he was missing and cause a furor over nothing. This seemed logical to Antius, so they relaxed at the top of the stern ladder to wait.

Moments later Charley came up the ladder and the three proceeded to the wheelhouse.

On the way back to the Temple, Antius indicated that he would like to know more about The Seeker and suggested that they might go again soon. Masters readily accepted the invitation, but also indicated that one of the crew members, perhaps Cliff, the engineer, should be taken along to give Antius a better and more complete description of the inner workings of the craft. Antius felt that this would be possible and left to make the arrangements for the tour. As soon as he left, Masters looked questioningly at Charley. "What did you find?" he asked.

"He's there, Mr. Reginald, but he's in a bad way. I don't think he's been out of his cabin. At least, that's the way it appears."

"What do you suggest?" Masters asked.

"Well, it's sure he's not going to listen to me. Maybe, if you or Mr. Alex…"

Masters creased his brow and muttered to himself. "I suggested that maybe we could bring Cliff along. If he could get Antius involved in the running of the ship, maybe I could talk to Davis. Too, I'd like to start those engines and see if they still are in good shape—perhaps Cliff could manage to do that as part of his demonstration."

"Charley," he said, "see if you can get Cliff to one side, preferably without any of the others around. Explain the situation to him and tell him that when we get on board, you and I are going to try to take care of the captain. Tell him, too, that I will want him to start the engines to check them out, but to do that we will need the soldiers aboard just to be safe. So, what I will want to do is have him show Antius about the engine room while you and I check the captain. When we return, we'll ask Antius to summon the soldiers and then, not before, we will start the engines. If there is any problem, then ask Cliff to see me. Okay?"

"Yes sir, Mr. Reginald."

Charley left Masters devising various plans to get everyone to the waterfront at the same time. He trusted Leila, but too many days had gone by without word and he could not just sit here and wait his turn on the altar, or whatever that high priest had planned for him.

A SUMMONS

The following morning after breakfast, Masters was summoned again before the High Priestess Naila. Other than the one moment at the Alliance, he still had not seen Leila and he wondered what this could be about. As he followed the soldier, he determined that this meeting with the lady would end somewhat differently from the last. It was clear that she had more authority than did Leila.

He was introduced much as before. However, this time she was seated and motioned him to a chair opposite her.

"Are you enjoying your stay in Encandor?" She spoke as though it were a short visit and a trace of a smile played around her coral lips.

"As much as can be expected under the circumstances." He paused, then continued, "You spoke as though it might not be an indefinite stay as your father, the High Priest, informed us earlier."

"There are certain possibilities." Again that trace of a smile.

"Possibilities?" Masters asked warily.

"For someone who stands in favor, yes," she replied.

Masters wondered exactly what she had in mind, but was hesitant to ask. After all, she might tell him and he might not like it. Then what would he do? So, he merely raised an eyebrow slightly as an indication of interest and said nothing.

"You are unlike the others who have come from your world before. It might be interesting to explore new vistas with you."

Still Masters said nothing. A tiny frown creased her forehead. This apparently was not going exactly as she had planned. However, Masters did not know what she was reaching for ... or, perhaps he did, but this was unfamiliar territory for him. He would have preferred to be on slightly firmer ground. However, nothing ventured, nothing gained. He decided to take the plunge. Perhaps this could be of help to him later.

"I was informed that there are no 'vistas' other than Encandor. Is that not correct?"

"Perhaps you spoke to one of limited scope?"

That was definitely a question! What was it she wanted to know? He decided to give her a little more information. "In one of the classes I attended, we were told that Encandor was the throne of Balim in the middle of the Lake of Kaos and that there was no other world. Do you, as a High Priestess of Balim, not agree?"

She frowned again. Aha. She did not like to be on the receiving end, he thought. Better be a little more careful. "Perhaps you could expound further on those new vistas of which you spoke." Now he smiled slightly. A little encouragement couldn't hurt.

"Even though not of Encandor, it is possible, should you prove yourself worthy, to attain certain heights." He thought her to be playing at words again. She sounded as though she were offering him a proposition or, rather, a challenge—one which was hard to refuse, but probably fatal to accept.

"What, exactly, would be required of me?" He asked.

"Ah, then you are interested?" She brightened visibly. He could not help but compare her with a cat ready to pounce on its victim. It was not a very comforting thought, but he must know more.

"Any man would be a fool to say no. You are a most beautiful woman—the High Priestess—you could offer much."

"I OFFER NOTHING."

Her manner instantly changed from a warm, sunny day to a cold, frosty night. Masters thought he had never before met a woman who could change moods so rapidly. But then, of course, he had never before met a high priestess.

"I apologize," he said immediately. "I did not mean to offend."

Her face softened. "Study on the words which I have spoken and we shall discuss it further tomorrow." She made as though to rise and Masters stood up quickly and offered his hand. As she accepted his aid, an icy chill ran up his spine. My God, her hand was as cold as death. It was all he could do to keep from shuddering. He was greatly relieved that the door opened at that moment and she dismissed him.

Antius had good news for Masters when he arrived back at his quarters. He would probably be busy all day tomorrow and, of course, would have to miss his next meeting with Naila. He was probably only putting off the inevitable, but he felt relieved nonetheless.

*   *   *

Each day, after the morning meal with her father and Naila, Leila performed those tasks assigned to her by D'Ar; then, for the balance of the day—until the evening meal, she was free to do pretty as much as she pleased. However, of late, she felt as though someone was watching her.

This morning, she had started toward the quarters of the otherworlders, hoping to see Masters. She thought him to be the handsomest of men and she particularly liked the sound of his voice. Her heart skipped a beat as she thought about him. She had just turned the corner into the last corridor and as she did she glanced behind her just in time to see a little whirl of blue disappear from sight. She had not passed anyone on the way here so she wondered whom it might be. Her caution made her turn and retrace her steps. When she reached the end of the corridor, she peaked around the corner and saw Naila's personal servant hastily retreating down the hall.

So, Naila WAS having her followed. She must be extra careful to avoid putting Masters, and his friends, at risk. She knew that Naila had a personal interest in him and there also was no need to put herself in jeopardy—too many times already had she felt Naila's anger.

This new turn of events frustrated her. There were many things she had wanted to learn of the otherworld and otherworlders. It was inconvenient that she now had to find other methods. Besides, she enjoyed this particular otherworlder and would like to spend more time with him. She let her thoughts drift now, wondering what it would be like to have his arms around her. It was with new determination that she turned now and walked briskly toward her own quarters. She decided that Naila would not deter her.

The very thought of deliberately defying Naila excited her; filled her with a delicious exhilaration. She felt in her heart that Masters was well worth any risk she might be taking.

After the evening meal, Leila once again visited Masters. This time, she took him to another part of the Temple where they were less likely to be seen.

"Naila has had me watched since the Presentation; thus, it took me longer to prepare for your escape."

"Are you really serious? I thought there was no escape from Encandor."

"Perhaps my choice of words was not exactly correct. From Encandor, there is no escape that we know of. Even D'Ar has come to the conclusion finally that the efforts in attempting to go into your world exact much too high a price. But within Encandor, that is a different matter."

"From? Within? I don't understand." He was truly puzzled.

"The secret society of which I spoke…?"

He nodded his acknowledgement.

"I have spoken with them. They have agreed to hide you for a short period of time. At this moment, they are preparing a place for you. It will be ready tomorrow."

"Tomorrow? This might be inconvenient. I am to take Antius back on board The Seeker. I see no way to get out of it."

Leila smiled at this last remark and it puzzled him somewhat.

"Antius is one of us. You need have no fear. I will speak with him in the morning."

Masters was excited at this news. "Does he know what you are planning?"

"Not yet. I had no idea he was involved with your group in any way. Why?"

"I was hoping to find some way of persuading him to let me start the engines tomorrow. If you could mention that to him, it would be most helpful. Of course, I know the soldiers guarding the boat will have to be present, but what I really want to do is test the engines, and Cliff Evans, our engineer, will be there also for added authenticity. And," he added as an afterthought, "Charley Washington will be with us, too."

"That will be perfect!" she exclaimed. "Antius can bring you to us after he has returned the others to their quarters. But, you will have to miss the evening meal." She laughed lightly. "You are strong enough. I think it will hurt you little to go without one meal."

He laughed, too. "You think that's funny, do you? In my world, we ate three meals each day. Of course, the days are longer there than here. For instance, we have been here thirteen of your days, but only eleven of ours."

She asked him then to tell her more of his world and, without realizing it, they spent several hours talking about the differences and similarities of his world and hers. In fact, they talked so long that Masters had just enough time to get back to his quarters to be summoned for the morning meal.

*   *   *

Masters had just finished a leisurely breakfast and was anticipating the day's events when trouble arrived in the form of Naila's personal servant. Oh, no! he thought. He had hoped to be away before she called for him.

He was conducted into the private sitting room of Naila's apartments. She was reclined on what appeared to be a chaise lounge, attired in a navy blue gauze robe which had slipped off her shoulder to partially reveal one breast. It was clasped at the waist with a golden serpent broach. That was appropriate, thought Masters. A perfectly shaped ivory leg peaked through a thigh-high slit. She wore gold slave chains on her ankles and her feet were bare.

She motioned to Masters to sit beside her and as she did so, the skirt of the robe slipped, revealing still more. Masters chose a chair opposite. Immediately, her expression changed to one of displeasure. As quickly as it had come, it was gone and she shrugged.

"Still the cautious one, I see. I mean you no harm. I merely wish to talk with you further."

"Well, let's talk." Masters was tired of this cat and mouse game, particularly since he was the mouse.

"Very well. I have reason to believe that there are subversive elements in Encandor who would overthrow D'Ar. It is quite possible that some of those very high in the Temple government are involved. You, as a stranger, could glean much information, as I'm sure you already have, and such information would be of great value to me." Her words were measured—speaking little, but saying much. "I would know now if you are interested. As you said yesterday, I could promise much."

She favored him with an alluring smile, but her eyes were cold and calculating. How unlike her sister she was, he thought.

"I'm willing to listen," he said casually. There could be no harm in that. Perhaps he could find out something here to help him and his friends.

"To listen is not enough. I must have a commitment from you."

Masters had to think quickly. To say no meant ill favor and who knew what. To say yes meant danger, excitement, adventure … but, what happened when she tired of her game. To say yes and betray her meant certain death if he were later caught. This certainly was a dilemma. Then, too, there was Leila. He was beginning to grow quite fond of her. Also, there was the question of gain. If he asked for too much … if he asked for too little… He did not wish to arouse her suspicions. He decided to play for time.

"If the reward were great enough…"

"And, what would a great enough reward for you?"

"I'm sure MY MISTRESS Naila could find a suitable reward for me." He must have placed the right amount of emphasis on the words because she smiled.

The slave chains tinkled as she swung her legs onto the floor. "You will dine with me this evening and I will tell you of my plan and of your reward."

He smiled as though in anticipation, but inwardly he was in turmoil. How was he going to handle this? He must find Leila somehow, perhaps through Antius, and tell her of these latest developments. He really had gotten himself in the middle of one hell of a situation here.

*   *   *

When Masters returned to his quarters, Antius, Cliff, and Charley were waiting for him. They were eager to get started and he had absolutely no chance to talk with Antius. He put Naila from his mind for the moment. He must see about the captain, who might be suffering from malnutrition if he hadn't eaten. That now was his prime concern.

They had an uneventful walk to the pier and, while Cliff was showing Antius the various mechanisms of The Seeker about which he had expressed an interest, Masters and Charley slipped away and went immediately to the captain's cabin. He was not there, so they had to search for him.

They found Davis in the galley drinking a cup of coffee. He explained that he had seen them approaching, so was not overly concerned with being found. His face was a little drawn, but other than that, he appeared to be okay. Before they left, Masters was determined to persuade him to eat more in the event of their escape.

Masters suggested that Charley check out the stores and make sure that nothing essential had been removed from the craft by those persons from Encandor who had previously toured the boat. If it was anything like home, he could expect to find half the boat missing. He told Charley to then go to the engine room where he would join him for the starting of the engines.

In the meantime, he filled Davis in on all that had transpired since their arrival—the Audience, the meetings with Naila and Leila, and lastly, the Presentation of Jennifer to Iltarn and, of course, the Alliance with Iltarn. He knew the captain had been very fond of Jennifer. He was surprised when the captain showed little interest in what had happened and no concern for Jen at all. When he broached the subject with Davis, Davis seemed somewhat disoriented. However, Davis, without appearing to have heard Masters at all, told him that, several evenings ago, he had been able to make a cursory inspection of the layout of the waterfront in between rounds of the soldiers who inspected the boat. He also told Masters that they seldom boarded The Seeker now and only walked down the pier once in about every five or six hours.

Masters then spoke with Davis about his health and urged him to maintain his strength, exacting a promise from Davis to eat more and to stop drinking. It would be an absolute necessity for him to be in the best possible condition when their escape attempt came since Davis was the only member of their party who had any freedom of movement at all and everything would depend on him to make sure The Seeker was ready and in good shape. As it now stood, they would try to escape in The Seeker to Mayran, the mainland. Even with cannibals, it probably would be no worse than here in Encandor and facing the likelihood of human sacrifice. It was not knowing for sure that bothered him the most.

Buoyed by this conversation with Masters and the possibility of getting his crew and passengers to relative safety, Davis assured Masters he could be counted on to be sober and ready for any contingency.

He took his leave of Davis, feeling that he had accomplished a little, if not all that he desired. Upon his arrival in the engine room, Antius suggested that they all go topside where he would signal the soldiers to come on board in order that Cliff might start the engines.

The starting of the engines went smoothly and Masters was pleased with the way Antius handled the soldiers. It was a relief to know that this pleasant young man was on their side. He would have liked to take her out for a run, but felt he had pressed his luck far enough for now.

It was about the middle of the afternoon—too early to return—so Antius asked if there was anything else they would like to see. Masters asked if it were possible to see the Temple craft which had brought them to Encandor, but was told this was out of the question. The Temple craft were well guarded and, other than when the strangers arrived, only soldiers in the service of D'Ar were permitted to enter therein.

Asked how many there were, Antius told them, "At one time there were many, seemingly filling the skies, but now there are three. Two are usually patrolling and one remains in the dock there." He pointed to the warehouse-type building from which the soldiers made their inspections of the pier.

"Why only three now?" Masters asked.

"Once our technology was great. And is now, in that we still have some of the machinery built by our forefathers. But, when it breaks down, there is none to service it—at least none who could be trusted to service it." He smiled and the portent of this statement was not lost upon Masters.

As they approached the Temple, Antius indicated that he would like to show Masters his collection of model boats from Masters' world and asked Cliff and Charley if they could find their way back to their quarters. They said they could, so he and Masters said their goodbyes and started off in another direction.

"Do you take me to Leila? I must speak with her at once. Naila has requested my presence at dinner tonight and I'm not sure just how to handle it."

Antius looked distressed. "Then we must hurry. We'll go directly to my apartment." They continued in the same direction, but at a much faster pace.

"I thought you lived in the Temple," Masters said.

"No," he answered. "Though most of the guides are of the Temple, not all are in the direct service of D'Ar. There are those of us who are in what you would call public relations. We mingle with the populace and make sure there are no subversives—that sort of thing."

Masters laughed. "You, a subversive, making sure there are no subversives."

By this time they had reached Antius' apartment. When they had entered, Antius went directly to a small niche in one wall. There he removed a small device which Masters was unable to identify. Antius depressed three small keys in a coded order and waited.

Mere seconds later, Masters heard Leila's voice. "Yes?" It was but a whisper.

Antius explained the situation quickly.

"By all means, he must keep the appointment with Naila. We cannot afford suspicions at this time. Tell him I will come to him afterwards with new arrangements."

Antius depressed one further key, returned the device to the niche and turned to Masters, a perfect picture of poise now that the crisis had passed. "Perhaps you would like to see my collection now."

"That's all there was to it? How did you get her so quickly?"

Now Antius laughed. "Your people really are quite primitive, you know. Here, persons in high places are equipped with sophisticated throat transceivers. I dialed Leila's personal code and she received my message direct. No go-betweens. No second ears—very private.

"We also have sophisticated mechanical devices," Masters countered, "but, as yet, we have seen no need to implant them in human beings. Although, I can see the value of it were you to be involved in a conspiracy."

After Antius had shown him his model collection, they strolled leisurely back to the Temple and when Masters reached his quarters, he found special clothing had been laid out for his "appointment" with Naila.

NAILA'S REWARD

Going to Naila's apartments was getting to be a habit. This time, however, he had a special honor guard. Also, he was dressed for the occasion—in blue. This was the first time he had seen blue on anyone other than those in the service of the Temple or those who ran the Temple. This suit was slightly different from the others in that the shirt was more of a blouse. It had full sleeves that ended in wide cuffs, a mandarin type collar, and a vee neck. The material was an iridescent royal blue that shone with greens and purples. The tight pants were of plain royal blue.

He was admitted by a servant girl dressed in a plain white robe. Naila was nowhere to be seen. When he had been seated in a comfortable chair, the girl offered him a choice of several beverages. He chose one of amber color in a pencil-thin glass. There was no way to actually drink from the glass, so he touched the edge with his tongue and tipped it upward. What a delightful flavor!

He was just raising the glass again when he heard a chimed melody. He looked up. Naila was entering the room. Perhaps this was not such a bad idea after all. She was a vision in flesh-colored chiffon, only slightly darker than her skin which peeked through her gown in the most intriguing places when she moved. Her hair was once again swept up in curls and glittered here and there with precious gems. A simple gold chain graced her throat. She wore ballerina-type gold mesh slippers. She literally floated across the room toward him.

He put down his glass and rose to greet her. Taking her hand in his, he bowed slightly and kissed her hand. He felt the same coldness as before and stifled an involuntary chill. It certainly took the glow off the evening in a hurry.

"Come, we will dine." She led him to still another room in the center of which were two lounge chairs with a small table between. He held her hand until she was comfortably seated, then reclined on the other lounge chair. He glanced around the room. Chiffon draperies in all colors of the rainbow and others in various shades of blue covered every wall and had been tied back only from the arch through which they had entered. Cushions were placed on the floor in various places about the room.

As soon as they were seated, the service began. Servant girls in white robes moved to and fro, but he had no time to check from whence they came as three girls dressed in scanty costumes entered. Two carried what appeared to be musical instruments and those two sat upon the cushions in one corner of the room. The third girl came over to the foot of the lounges, curtsied deeply, turned her back and, raising her arms above her head, snapped her fingers. The music began and Masters witnessed the most sensuous dance he had ever seen.

Naila had prepared the evening well—the food was delicious, the beverages tasty and warming, the dancing most moving. The only thing that took the edge off was the coldness of her touch. He wondered just what she expected of him. He hoped it was not the obvious.

After dinner, the dancing girl and musicians dismissed and the table removed, Naila smiled. "What think you of our hospitality now?" There was a deceptive warmth in her voice.

"I think this is a part of Encandor I could learn to like a lot. This is certainly not the soldiers' fare."

A young woman of about nineteen years entered the room carrying a gold tray with two of the pencil-thin glasses of the amber liquid he had sampled earlier. She offered one to Naila and as Naila took the glass she said, "This is Nubia, a Virgin of Balim. Her life is dedicated to his service."

The girl turned to offer the second glass to Masters. She had the exquisite features of a china doll and her skin was a golden tan. Her gown, of a Grecian style, was of the palest blue chiffon; the top was only a single layer and her young breasts stood proud and firm—the skirt fell to the floor in many folds. As she leaned over to offer him the drink, her dark hair fell forward, just long enough to cover the tips of her breasts. As she leaned close to him, the scent of musk filled his nostrils. A half smile, sweet and innocent, revealed even white teeth.

Taking the proffered glass, he raised it in a toast, "Nubia," and touched it to his tongue.

Naila dismissed the girl and then, much like Leila, she asked him about the different customs of his world and, as they talked, a languor came over him. He tried half-heartedly to shake it off. It probably was a combination of the drink and a sleepless night. He determined not to drink any more tonight. Through hazy vision, he saw Naila rise from her couch and started to rise himself, but she motioned him to remain and she left the room. He leaned his head against the back of the couch for what seemed but a moment, when he felt a hand on his shoulder. He opened his eyes expecting to see Naila, but instead it was Nubia.

"You are tired." Her voice was musical, thrilling and sounded like a cool breeze on a summer night. "My mistress Naila has had a room prepared for you." She took him by the hand, not the coldness of Naila, rather the warmth of a heady wine. It seemed to revitalize him somewhat. He was not too surprised when she led him into a richly appointed bedroom and closed the door behind them.

*   *   *

Releasing his hand, she moved toward the bed and turned back the covers. She then returned to Masters and led him to the bed, where he sat on the edge. She deftly removed his clothing and he fell back on the bed, ready to sleep. But this was not to be. Nubia gracefully mounted the bed and, in a kneeling position, silently and with downcast eyes—almost shyly—she slipped from her gown. She looked over at him but his eyes were closed. She could not let it end this way; her mistress had given her instructions and were they not followed, there would be severe repercussions. She had felt Naila's anger before and did not wish a recurrence.

Masters had wanted only to retire when she led him in here and it appeared that he would get his wish but the girl first put her fingers on his Temples and massaged them lightly, then moved on down to his face. He opened his eyes and, for the first time, realized what she was doing. He was exhausted and tried to ignore the fact that she was offering herself to him but she would not leave him alone.

She continued her gentle massaging as she moved her hands down to his chest, then she leaned over and, with her tongue, she gently nudged one tiny nipple while pinching the other. He thought briefly of Leila and made an extraordinary effort to push Nubia away but she would not go. Instead, she moved her hands down the trunk of his body until she reached his genitals. He was simply too tired and thoughts of Leila kept coming into his mind. Why wouldn't she, Nubia, just go away? Instead, she wound her fingers in the hair and pulled until she was sure he was at least partially awake, all the while she was using her tongue to trace a pattern down his slim, hard belly. By this time, Masters had roused himself enough, tired as he was, to be aroused and when she put her hot mouth on his cock, he was wide awake.

This was a VIRGIN? What did they teach these girls in the service of the Temple? Whatever it was, this girl was GOOD! It appeared futile to resist, nor did he want to. However, just then, another picture of Leila with a slight frown came to mind. This was too much AND he was very, very tired, so with one last desperate move, he pushed Nubia away and turned over. It was then that she began to sob. He turned once more toward her. She was on her knees in the middle of the bed. He wanted to console her but feared once more becoming out-of-control. He reached up to touch her with one hand and she turn tear-filled eyes toward him. "My mistress will be so very angry with me because I have failed."

He sat up and took her into his arms. He held her this way and simply explained the situation to her. No one need ever know. He certainly would not tell her mistress but, right now, he simply wanted to sleep. He lay back then and closed his eyes in sleep.

* * *

Perrin leaned back on the lounge chair. He had just finished the evening meal and was relaxing. It would have been nice to have a cigarette, but he had not seen anyone smoke since their arrival.

He mused to himself on what had happened since that fateful day in the North Atlantic of that other world. He never was overly adventurous as was his friend Masters. He never shied away from the unknown or trouble, but he would never deliberately seek it out. Now he wished himself back on board The Seeker with its familiarity and the security of his own world.

In the past, he had many times found that the best medicine for this type of problem was to keep himself busy, which is exactly what he had done the past several days, going on several tours of the city, visiting museums and art galleries. On his second tour he had met Delia, who was most informative about the music and art of Encandor. She seemed to share his interests and so he had requested her services on all future tours.

She had taken him to a concert on their second tour. He found the music strangely compelling, drawing him into a primitive state unlike anything he had experienced before. When he questioned Delia about this, she was somewhat evasive, stating that she did not feel primitive when she heard the music.

This afternoon, she had taken him to a special art gallery. It was quite an experience. For the most part, at least from what he had seen up to now, the art was the same, or at least similar, to that at home, but in this gallery it was different. Each work of art was in its own special cubicle, which was large enough to hold four or five observers at one time. While the work was being viewed, an historical squib about the artist and his work was given in a pleasant voice. Then, through some technology, the viewer was in the art work itself, experiencing sight, sound, smell, touch, and taste. Most particularly he was fascinated by one scene—a seascape—where it was so real, he could even taste the salt air.

When the viewing was over, he questioned Delia about the location of this particular painting. All she would tell him was that it was on the other side of the world. He asked her what she meant by that, but she refused to expound further. He was insistent, which seemed to upset her greatly, to the point that she had canceled their date to go to a concert this evening, leaving their relationship hanging in mid air; which is why he was here now. He had wanted to call her, but had no way of getting in touch with her.

Thinking about Delia now made him restless and he decided to go for a walk. The night was cool, but comfortable, and as he left the building, he turned towards the waterfront. For some reason, he felt compelled in that direction. Of all the places he had been, up to this moment he had avoided the waterfront. Knowing that he could not return to his world, he refused to knowingly torture himself.

As he walked along, he felt the hair at the back of his neck prickle. He could not put his finger on it, but something was not quite right. He continued on at the same pace, but he turned right at the next corner. As the feeling persisted, he quickened his pace and turned right again, heading back toward the Temple. He had no idea what the feeling meant—whether someone was following him or if some danger lay ahead; perhaps even the danger lay back at the Temple, but he felt that it would be best to be with his friends.

During the entire walk, he encountered no one, but still the feeling was there. Something was wrong, but he had no idea what. He entered the door to his quarters; no one was in sight. He called out to his friends, but received no answer. He checked each of the rooms—no one. He had just sat down on the edge of his bed when he heard the door to the common room open and Sim's voice. He was conversing with someone.

Quietly Perrin stepped to the door and checked the outer room. Martin and Barron were there. He stepped forward as to enter the room when he heard a knock on the door. Barron opened the door to reveal three soldiers. One of the soldiers had his weapon drawn and pointed in the direction of Sim Barron; the others were standing at ready.

"What are you doing? What's going on?" Sim demanded.

The soldiers pushed Barron back into the room and entered behind him.

Perrin quickly, but quietly, stepped back into his own room, removed a pencil and note pad from his pocket and hastily penned a note, partially slipping it under Masters' pillow. He then returned the pad and pencil to his pocket and deliberately lay back on the bed and closed his eyes as though he were asleep.

A sharp jab in the ribs brought an involuntary cry of pain. Perrin opened his eyes to see a soldier standing menacingly over him with his weapon drawn. He indicated that Perrin should rise from the bed and join the others in the outer room. When he entered the outer room, Perrin saw that Barron and Martin were still held at gunpoint. He wanted to question the soldiers, but Barron had tried to no avail.

"Gentlemen," he said, looking at Martin and Barron, "I think our destiny has caught up with us. Shall we march to meet it?"

The soldier behind him apparently did not appreciate his wry humor, as he shoved his weapon in Perrin's back and gave him a hard push toward the door.

*   *   *

December 19, …

Naila was pleased about last night. She felt she had Masters exactly where she wanted him—she had found his weakness. Nubia's report was very promising and Naila had told her to visit

Masters each night in his quarters. She smiled at the thought of what she had done. Now, for her instructions to Nikto.

"Nikto, there will be no question; no argument. You will carry out your orders as I have given them. This man Masters is not to be trusted, though he will have certain privileges. You will see that he has a personal transceiver coded to you and you will let me know where he goes and what he does on a daily basis. He MUST report to you daily. Is that understood?"

Nikto nodded. He definitely was not happy about this turn of events. He liked Masters and was sorry to see that he had fallen under Naila's spell.

She continued, "Nubia will take care of the nights." This last was said with unabashed gloating.

*   *   *

When Masters woke, cotton in his mouth and alone, he felt that, somehow, he had betrayed Leila's trust. Not that he had made any promise to her nor had he even looked at her in any way but as a friend; in fact, he really had done nothing but sleep and, right now, he was unsure, however, how he even felt about her. He WAS sure, however, how he felt about Naila and her request that he betray Leila and her friends and he still did not know just how he was going to handle this particular problem. He glanced around the room. The fancy clothes were gone and in their place the familiar green uniform. He found the bathroom and quickly showered and shaved. He had barely completed dressing when a soldier entered. Was there no privacy in this place? Nobody ever seemed to knock.

He was conducted again into Naila's presence—this time in what appeared to be an office. She was seated behind a small desk and indicated that he sit in one of the chairs opposite her.

She waited until he was seated, then "I trust you spent a pleasant night." Her voice was crisp and businesslike. "As I told you earlier, I have reason to believe there are certain subversive elements in Encandor and you, as a stranger, would be in a much better position to obtain information about them than would I. Were you to agree to obtain this information, I could place at your disposal the many resources of Encandor and, should you be successful…" She hesitated here as though she expected Masters to speak, then continued, "I am sure there are many things you would find pleasing to your taste. They would be yours for the asking."

"Greeks bearing gifts?" Masters quipped.

Naila frowned her misunderstanding, then "If that is what you wish and it is in our power to provide."

Masters thought he had better quit while he was ahead. "We can speak of that AFTER the fact. If I understand you correctly, that is when the reward comes; after the information is obtained… right?"

"There are certain aspects of the Temple which you may enjoy while the investigation is in process." Again, she looked like the proverbial cat, and there was no doubt as to what she meant. "However, you must decide now." She was all business again.

Now that he realized there was to be no personal relationship between them, Masters decided to play it out. "I am at your service."

She rose. "Good. Nikto will furnish you with the details. He will give you your instructions and provide you with whatever you need. Masters could not help but note the confidence in her attitude and a faint trace of malicious pleasure in her voice, as though she had expected this result all along. She touched her throat. "Nikto."

The door opened and Masters turned in his chair to see Nikto walk in and bow slightly to Naila.

"You will give Masters his instructions and provide for his needs as we discussed earlier. I will expect your reports on a daily basis." Then to Masters, "You will report directly to Nikto and he will report to me."

Nikto nodded his agreement as Naila sat down and turned to other matters on her desk. "Come," he said to Masters. "We will take the morning meal together."

*   *   *

All during breakfast, Nikto made small talk and seemed to carefully avoid saying anything about Naila's instructions. Masters wanted to get it over with and be on his way, so he decided to take the bull by the horns.

"Nikto, you seem reluctant to give me Naila's instructions. Is anything wrong?"

"Masters," Nikto began, "are you absolutely sure you want to go through with this? Naila is a very powerful woman and I would not like to see you hurt. Also, there is the matter of Leila. She is much taken with you. As yet, Naila does not know. Should she learn of it, however..." He paused.

"Sibling rivalry?"

"Not exactly." He paused again, as though trying to choose his words very carefully. "Naila has always had her father's favor. She learned to wield her power at his knee. She revels in it. On the other hand, Leila is the gentle one and it pleases Naila to hurt her."

He went on to tell Masters of the last Day of Sacrifice— when Masters and his group arrived—and of how Naila had persuaded D'Ar to use Leila's best friend, even though her time had not yet come.

He stopped, as though he had said too much, then rushed on, "Naila has her good points, too. It is just that her father gave her too much power too early."

"Do you love her?"

"An Alliance with Naila would do well for me; however, I am not unaware of her faults."

"Nikto, I'm going to have to trust you. You can either betray me or help me. I'm banking on the latter."

"I don't understand." Nikto was clearly puzzled.

Masters explained his ideas for escape, carefully avoiding any mention of Leila or her secret society. He did not trust Nikto that far. He did, however, need to know how far Nikto would go to gain a clear field with his mistress, and also just how much he would do in her behalf. Ambition had moved stronger men to do hideous things, and Masters did not want to find out at the last moment that Nikto's ambition was as chilling as Naila's touch.

However, he need not have worried. As he explained his plans, Nikto brightened. And, too, Nikto had a few ideas of his own. It seemed he was all too glad to have Masters out of his way completely, even at certain risks to himself.

By the time they had finished, it was nearly noon. Nikto had explained to Masters that Naila had wanted him to have the freedom of Encandor and whatever resources were necessary and had agreed to equip him with a special communications device. (It turned out to be the same as the one he had seen earlier in Antius' apartment—although he made no mention of this to Nikto.) Nikto was also to give Masters his own special code so Masters could reach him at any time should he require anything further or have anything to report.

He cautioned Masters, however, that until his escape plans were actually put into effect, daily progress reports were imperative. And he had best find something favorable to report. Naila was no fool and Temple spies were everywhere. Everything must be circumspect.

Naila had also suggested that perhaps new clothing should be provided Masters, but Masters declined, saying that he felt he would be too conspicuous in blue. What he had would do very nicely. Nikto agreed.

Nikto then left to make the arrangements for the items Masters had requested and Masters went back to his quarters to begin implementation of his plans.

When he arrived, Masters found his quarters deserted. This was most unusual. Usually there were at least some servants around doing various chores. He checked his and Perrin's room. Nothing. No, wait. What was that? He noticed a scrap of paper peeking from under his pillow. Pulling it out, he found it was a hastily scribbled note. "They have taken us. A" What could it mean? He rushed through the common room and into the corridor. He quickly glanced one way, then the other. No one was in sight. He forced himself to stop and think. What did he really expect to find? The soldiers carrying his friends away? No, this must have been planned earlier—much earlier. He had no idea when they might have been taken away. It could have been an hour ago, or it could have been last night after he left for his appointment with Naila.

He wondered if this might not be Naila's doing. Nikto should be here soon. Maybe he would have the answer. He was pacing up and down the corridor, still holding the note, when Nikto arrived.

"Just what is the meaning of this?" he asked as he shoved the note into Nikto's face.

Nikto took the note and looked at it, first one way and then another. "I don't understand. What is it?"

"WHAT IS IT? Just read it."

"I cannot read your language."

Immediately contrite at his error, Masters told Nikto what the note said, at the same time demanding to know where his friends had been taken and why.

Nikto appeared to be as puzzled as he. "This is the first I knew of this. But, it appears that Naila has taken out what you call a little 'insurance' on her plans for you."

Masters stood there, helpless in his anger, with his fists clenched at his sides. "She can't do this to me. I'll find a way to…"

Nikto put a friendly hand on Masters' shoulder. "My friend," he said, "I will help you find your companions, but for now you must follow through on our discussion of this morning. Here, I have brought the communicator. I will show you how to use it and give you my personal code. You can reach me at any time, day or night. I assure you, I will help you find your friends."

He led a reluctant Masters back into his quarters. "Before I do anything," Masters said, "I wish to know my friends are safe. If one of them is harmed…"

"And what will you do? Please understand, I am on your side, but certainly you must realize by now that, at best, your position in Encandor is a precarious one. I have promised you my help. I can do no more. Now, you must help yourself—and your friends—by doing that which you promised."

"Very well. If you will provide me with a guide, I'll get started," Masters said, but without conviction.

"You no longer require a guide. You are free to go anywhere you choose."

Masters was taken aback. "Even aboard The Seeker?"

"Even aboard The Seeker, if that is your wish. However, should you lose your bearings while you are exploring, just call me on the communicator and I will direct you back to the Temple. Encandor is not too large, but you still can get lost easily. Remember, too, that as long as you report daily, your friends will be safe enough; but should you not report, do not depend on Naila's kindheartedness. I'm afraid you will find it lacking.

"I must go now, as I have other duties." He grasped Masters' hand in a silent acknowledgement of friendship, then left the room.

Masters was unsure exactly how to begin this project he had so glibly agreed to earlier today. But start he must. He would like to speak with Leila but did not know how to get in touch with her. Or, maybe he did. But, he must take some precautions. First, he tucked the communicator under his pillow and smoothed the covers on the bed—no point in taking chances that the communicator was bugged—then he felt all over his clothing to see if some device had possibly been planted there. He found nothing but, of course, there could be one and he missed it. He left the Temple feeling better than he had in days. At least now he had a semblance of a plan of action.

*   *   *

Nikto left Masters intending to go about his duties. His footsteps, however, carried him once again to the observation room and his fingers coded in the desired numbers as though with a mind of their own.

Tiffany's form leapt into view. He never ceased to marvel at the many, many moods of this beautiful woman. Each time he came here—and there were many—she presented a totally different picture. He wondered now how he could have even considered an Alliance with Naila and Masters' question about love … well, he knew that he had never been in love with Naila. He was unsure even now that what he felt for Tiffany was akin to love. After all, he had never spoken with the woman, although the desire was strong.

A PLAN FOR ESCAPE

Antius opened the door at the first knock. "I am glad you finally got here. We were beginning to worry. Leila tried to contact you last evening and found your quarters deserted. Nor could she learn where you and your friends had been taken. What happened."

"Apparently Naila has plans for me and is using my friends as hostages against my failure to do her bidding. Nikto is trying to find out where they are located now."

"Nikto? By the Eye of Balim! Don't you know that he will do anything for Naila? He's had his eye on an Alliance with her for a long, long time. How can you even THINK of trusting him?"

"I know he is ambitious, but I trust him. I have a very strong feeling of friendship for him and believe that he will help us to escape from here if it's possible to escape. I don't know exactly why he's willing to help, but I believe in him and I trust him."

He related to Antius all that had taken place between him and Naila and Nikto. "He has given me a personal communicator with his special code so that I may contact him at any time."

Antius was aghast. "You have led them right to my door."

"Not unless there is a bug on me that I couldn't find."

"No, no. The communicator. Once activated with his code, Nikto can trace you anywhere."

"If that's all, you need not worry. I didn't bring it with me. I left it at the Temple."

Antius looked instantly relieved.

I came here to contact Leila. I would like to speak with her. She told me she had some sort of plan, but I'm sure things have changed now, with my friends in Naila's control. Can you take me to her? Or bring her here?"

"She must not come here. We will meet her later this evening as originally planned for yesterday. You will meet some of our group and we can formulate our plans from there. Of course, we will have a place for you to stay."

"But I must report to Nikto daily so that he, in turn, can report to Naila on my progress. If I do not, my friends will be in jeopardy."

"We will provide you with a communicator—one with a scrambler so that you can transmit safely. We will also provide you with the information to relay to Nikto so that Naila will not question your loyalty to your friends. Come, we will have a drink to your successful escape, then you may rest until it is time."

This left Masters somewhat less than satisfied. He had wished to see Leila right away, but he accepted the drink from Antius with as much good humor as he could muster, and leaned back in his chair.

*   *   *

He didn't want to wake up; he was comfortable and in the middle of a fantastic dream. But someone kept rocking the boat; threatening to turn it over.

"Masters, wake up! It is time!"

"Leila?" Leila! He sat up, immediately awake. He looked around the room. There she was. She and Antius and about half a dozen others whom he had not seen before; in a place he had not seen before; and he was in clothes he had not seen before. Who had changed his clothes? And how had he gotten here? Then he remembered the drink.

"Antius, you slipped me a Mickey. Between Naila and you, I guess I'm going to have to give up drinking while I'm here."

"Mickey?" Antius looked puzzled. "What's a Mickey?"

"It means you put something in my drink to knock me out. And, I'm not sure I appreciate it."

Antius smiled. "I put nothing in your drink. I merely gave you a taste of the Anderdust."

"What is that?"

"It is a drink made from the Ander, a bush which grows profusely here in Encandor. It does not affect us as it does otherworlders. We felt you needed rest for what is ahead. Your part in our plans is not going to be easy."

He quickly introduced Masters to the two women, Antina and Delia, and five men, Manar, Filius, Batiel, Drosar, and Landar. "There are others, but we do not all meet at the same time for our own protection. For the present, this is the group that will work with you on the matter of your return to your world."

"Return? You mean there is a possibility we can return? I thought…"

"We don't know if you can return." This was the woman Delia. "However, we can try. It will be very dangerous. You will be exposed to the Eye of Balim. Not very many survive unscathed who look upon it."

"I'll try anything!"

"It will not be just you. Your friends will also have to agree. And you will be risking your craft as well. Should that be destroyed, so would your probability of escape, even to Mayran."

"They will feel the same as I do. But, of course, they will have to be given a choice—to go or not. Although, I feel there is not much choice between death at sea; death on land; your fancy god's altar; slavery. None of it sounds really appealing, but at least we will have a chance, and we will be doing something, instead of just sitting around waiting."

"Those are not the only alternatives. There IS Mayran." It was Leila who now spoke.

"And there, death at the hands of cannibals? Thanks, but no thanks."

"Not necessarily death…" she began, but Delia put a hand on her arm.

"There is time to talk of Mayran when all else has failed. Then, of course, we could always return him to the Temple and Naila." This she said with a sly smile.

"Delia, no! You know what my sister is like." She turned to Masters. "There can be safety on Mayran, should you choose that way."

"I would first like to try to get back to my own world. Any other choice would have to be secondary." He looked directly into her eyes. "You do understand, don't you?"

She nodded, but she did not look very happy about his decision. "Of course. Delia will explain the possibilities and the dangers involved in her plan." She inclined her head in Delia's direction.

Delia explained that on the next Day of Sacrifice, The Seeker would have to be in exactly the same position as when it arrived. Only in that way could there be any chance of success in her plan.

"Antius has told us that your ship is in good condition, but does not know how much pressure it can stand. You understand, I hope, that when D'Ar turns the key and the explosion occurs..." At this remark, Masters looked at her questioningly. "Yes, explosion—a very powerful explosion—not unlike one of your own weapons, I believe, but under water and with considerably more direction. When this explosion occurs, it displaces some of the water in the Lake of Kaos and throws it skyward to where, we believe, it joins with your world in a sort of ... rip in space, for want of a better description; then it settles back into the Lake. This 'rip in space' is open for only a short period of time, a few moments at most.

"As in your case, if there are any craft from your world in that immediate area, they are sucked down into the vortex of a maelstrom created by this 'rip' which ties your world to ours. And that is why there is no way back. However, if your craft is above the exact spot when the explosion occurs, there is a slight, and I must emphasize SLIGHT, possibility that at the exact moment when the rip occurs, your craft may be forced upward and back into your own world. Of course, you realize, there is no guarantee that the maelstrom will not drag you down again even should you be successful in being in the right place at the right time; and provided also that the explosion does not demolish your craft.

"Then, too, there is the danger of radiation, should you survive the explosion, and the blinding light that accompanies the explosion. These you must be protected from in advance. The maelstrom—well, there is really no protection from that or the initial explosion. We must hope that you will be thrown clear on the other side. It is a slim hope, at best."

"But one we must try," said Masters, "just as soon as we can get all of my people together."

"I would go with you!" The words were spoken very quietly, but most fervently.

"Leila, I cannot be responsible for your safety. It is too dangerous. You must stay in your own world. Don't you see that there is nothing here for us, but you have your whole life before you."

"I WILL GO!" She seemed as determined to go as he was for her to stay. She apparently had been used to getting her own way.

But not this time. "No. There is no point in speaking of it further. You will stay."

She turned, then, and promptly left the room.

He was immediately sorry that he had spoken to her so harshly. "Leila," he called. But she did not return.

He forced his mind to other matters. "How will we get my friends out of Naila's hands? How long until the next Day of Sacrifice? And, what of Jennifer?"

Delia held up her hand to stop his flow of words. "Hold! The Day of Sacrifice is thirteen days hence. And, as we did not know that your friends would be taken, we had not planned on this particular contingency; nor did we know that Naila would be keeping her eye on you. That makes things a little more difficult. For now, however, you must make your report to Nikto. Antius will brief you. Then, it will probably be best for you to go back to the Temple to avoid suspicion and, perhaps, gain further information on the whereabouts of your friends.

Thus far, we have had no success in locating them. We will be in touch with you."

It was a somewhat dejected Masters who returned to the Temple that evening. Antius had given him the information to transmit to Nikto, returned his clothes, put him in an aircar that would bring him to the place where Nikto had first brought him into the Temple, then bade him goodbye. Things could not get much worse, what with Jennifer in the Palace; Perrin and the others in Naila's hands; and he hadn't seen Tiffany or Helen since the day of the audience with D'Ar almost two weeks ago—and now Leila had walked out and he couldn't even talk to her.

To top it all off, he had missed dinner. But, Leila had promised him that, hadn't she?

He opened the door to his bedroom and found Nubia there. That was probably Naila's work. Well, he was in no mood for that sort of thing right now, and sent her away, after which he took out the communicator and keyed in Nikto's code to relay his first report.

*   *   *

Leila had been outside Masters' room when Nubia had entered. She stayed in the shadows for a short while, debating in her mind just what to do, when Masters arrived. Delia had said he was to return to the Temple, but she had not planned on Nubia. Now her plans would be ruined. She was just about to leave when the door opened and Masters ushered Nubia out.

Delighted with this turn of events, she waited until Nubia was out of sight, then quietly opened the door of Masters' suite and entered. He was in the bedroom talking. To whom, she wondered. She tiptoed to the bedroom door and peeked in. Greatly relieved, she saw that he was only speaking into a communicator and heard Nikto's voice in reply. Only his report. She stood quietly until he signed off and, as he was leaning over the bed to replace the communicator, she silently moved up behind him and placed her hands on his hips.

127

He whirled around. "I thought I..." he began angrily.

Leila was caught off balance and fell to the floor with a little yelp.

When Masters saw it was she, his mood changed immediately. He bent over, picked her up and laid her gently on the bed, then knelt down beside the bed on one knee.

"I'm sorry. I thought it was..."

She put a finger to his lips. "It is all right. I should have made my presence known."

A thousand thoughts rushed through his head and he looked down at her lying there. She looked so small and helpless, albeit every inch a princess. He slowly moved forward and gathered her into his arms. She offered no resistance, but neither did she respond. He held her for a moment, then released her gently back onto the pillow.

"Just what are you doing here? When you left today..."

"I was angry. But you were right. My place is here. Enough of that. I thought you might be hungry, so I had a small meal prepared for us." She started to rise and he helped her up. "Come," she said.

He had not released her hand, so they walked hand in hand to the apartment where she had taken him before when they had spent the whole night talking. There, a simple table had been set between two lounge chairs much in the same manner as had been Naila's dinner. They ate in silence, glancing now and again at each other. When they had finished, a serving girl removed the table and Masters leaned back and relaxed.

"What was Nubia doing in your room?"

The question took Masters by surprise and he didn't quite know how to answer.

"Well?"

"I think, possibly, she was a bribe from Naila in return for my being a 'good boy.'"

"Good boy? What does that mean?"

"In this case, it means doing whatever Naila wants me to do."

"And did you?"

"Did I what?"

"Do what Naila wanted?"

"Not yet. I hope never to have to."

This seemed to satisfy her and Masters hoped she would not pursue the subject of Nubia. He did not wish to tell the truth, nor did he wish to lie to this girl. Now that he thought on it, he was at a loss to understand just why he cared whether or not she was hurt, but care he did. Then he brushed it from his mind. It did not really matter too much whether he cared or not, for in a few days he and his friends would be on their way out of here—he hoped—and he would probably never see her again.

All this while, Leila had sat quietly watching him. Now, she rose and took his hand, silently bidding him to rise, and led him to a room, in the center of which was a curtained bed. Just inside the door, she turned and reached up, pulling his head gently down, and placed her lips on his. The kiss began most tenderly, like a taste of honey, then, as passion mounted, like an electric shock. He picked her up and carried her to the bed. Tearing aside the curtains, he broke their embrace and dropped her unceremoniously on the bed, turned and strode quickly from the room.

He had made a momentous discovery. He loved this girl! And he had made an instant decision—he could not take her like this. As much as he wanted her, he wanted something better for her.

He went out into the cool night air and when he finally returned to his room, he heard the Morning Chimes.

*   *   *

Leila watched him leave through tear-dimmed eyes. She was not able even to do this right! She saw her last hope of either holding him here, or going with him, disappear as he just had.

129

*   *   *

December 22, …

For the next several days, Masters heard nothing from Leila or her friends, other than the daily reports from Antius, who assured him that some progress was being made, but as yet no one knew where his friends were.

During this time, he had acquainted himself with Encandor as much as possible, only once getting lost and having to call upon Nikto. And, just today, he had made another trip to The Seeker and was surprised that no one stopped him. He had a long talk with the captain over a cup of coffee and explained the plans for escape. Davis seemed willing enough to try and Masters felt sure the others would be willing also, if he could just find them.

Strolling back to the Temple, he glanced at his watch. The date read "22." He had been much too busy to think about it before, but this was one hell of a way to spend Christmas. If the escape plans did not work, he had better get used to it.

He stopped by Antius' apartment for his report and stayed for the evening meal. They chatted for a while and Masters helped Antius on his model of The Seeker, putting in some detailing on the deck.

It was a clear evening and, although there was no moon over Encandor, there was an ever-present glow and Masters had no trouble finding his way back to the Temple. He wondered idly if Nubia would be in his quarters. She had been there every evening, and every evening he had put her out. Since his last encounter with Leila, he had been interested in no one else. He wondered if Nubia had reported all this to her mistress and, if so, what Naila might think. Thus far, he did not even know if she was satisfied with his reports; and at the end of each of those reports he had asked of his friends, but Nikto had declined to discuss the matter.

He was greatly relieved to find the apartment empty and, after he finished his report, he lay back on the bed, still fully clothed, with his arms behind his head. He wondered if these people had anything in the way of entertainment, like television. So far, there had been no evidence of it. Actually, he had seen very little for anyone here to be too happy about or to celebrate. It was no wonder they were trying to change it. He started to doze.

"Masters!"

He smiled in his half-sleep. It was Leila.

"Masters!" The voice was insistent.

He opened his eyes, but there was no one there. He must have been dreaming.

"Masters, wake up!"

It WAS Leila. He sat up.

"Yes?"

"Meet me in the apartment. I have news for you. Can you find it?"

"Yes."

He got up, splashed water on his face and ran a comb through his hair. What news? Maybe it was about Perrin and the others. He wasted little time getting to the apartment.

She opened the door just as he arrived and closed it immediately after him.

"What's your news?" he asked anxiously, afraid of the worst.

"First of all, I have located your friends. They are safe for the moment. It will not be easy to get them out, but I think it can be managed. But, too, there is bad news. Your friend Tiffany is to be the next bride to honor Balim." The words just spilled out, like milk from an overturned glass.

He was stunned. Tiffany? He grasped her roughly by the shoulders. "We must stop him. He can't do this. He can't just go around killing people at a whim. Who does he think he is anyway?"

He saw tears form in her eyes and realized that he was hurting her, but she said nothing. He released her. "I'm sorry. For a moment, I forgot he was your father."

She rubbed her shoulders and smiled through her tears at his error. "The tears were not for my father, but for the strength of your hands."

"Oh, damn," he said between his teeth and tenderly embraced her to relieve her pain. She remained in his arms for a moment or so, then slowly put her arms around him.

"Masters, I am truly sorry about your friends. I did not know until today that this was planned. Now it is too late for, without the sacrifice, there is no chance of return for you at all. I would offer myself in her stead, were it possible."

This time he knew there was no turning back. He knew she loved him, too, and he picked her up and carried her into the bedroom. He placed her gently on the bed.

He leaned back slightly. "Leila, I know there is no true future for us but I love you more than life. You know, too, that I must try to escape back to my world and that you must stay here. Can you accept the NOW with no regrets?"

Her answer was to reach for him and pull him to her.

*   *   *

"I care not for your opinion. What are the otherworlders to me—or to you, for that matter?"

Naila lifted her chin ever so slightly and, though Nikto was fully a foot taller than she, she managed to look down upon him. She had just informed him that Tiffany—his Tiffany—his beautiful, black-haired Tiffany—was to grace the Altar of Balim in four days' time, and she could not be swayed to use another.

He was distraught as he now strode purposefully down the corridor. He had just left Naila's apartments and he fervently hoped she had not seen his shock and discomfort at the news.

He went immediately to the observation room and turned on the cameras. Tiffany was asleep on the bed. Her disheveled hair formed a halo around her face.

He turned on the communication device. "Tiffany," he called softly so as not to startle her. He called again. She stirred slightly, a tiny frown creasing her forehead. He called again. This time she opened her eyes and looked about the room.

"Tiffany, please do not be frightened. No harm will come to you. I am Nikto. You will remember me from the boarding."

She still looked a little puzzled, but nodded affirmation.

Briefly, he told her the news of her friends and what had transpired since their arrival. Then, as gently as possible, he explained the path her own future was to take.

"I will, of course, be close at hand at all times and should the opportunity present itself, I will take you away from this place. I ask that you trust me and say nothing of this to your friend. She is in no immediate peril."

She whispered "Thank you," and, although her expression did not change, he saw tears start to form in her eyes.

"Remember, I will be nearby, my beautiful princess." Before she could say or do anything, he switched off the camera and microphone. As he leaned back in the chair, he realized his heart was pounding. What had he done? If he kept his promise to this girl to rescue her, fail or succeed, he would sign his own death warrant. D'Ar would have no compassion, whatever the reason. And Naila, wouldn't she have just loved this scene? What she could do to make his life a torment would be worse than death on the Altar of Balim.

But he had never gone back on his word, and, if it were at all possible, whatever the consequences, he did not intend to do so this time.

*   *   *

The following morning at breakfast, Nikto relayed the same information to Masters that he had received from Leila with one small addition. Naila had moved up the Day of Sacrifice. Originally, it would have been on December 28. It was now to be December 26. He asked why but Nikto was loathe to discuss the matter. Masters did not press him—perhaps he had some personal reason for his silence. He had asked Nikto then just how much help he could expect in obtaining the release of his friends.

"All I am able to do is not deter you. The only possible time will be on the Day of Sacrifice. I will order the regular guards to attend the rites and will simply fail to replace them. I will also provide you with the exact location where your friends are being held and the best avenues of escape from there."

"There is one further favor," Masters said. "I will also need the coordinates of The Seeker when she arrived here."

"But why will you need that?"

"I intend to try to return to my own world."

"But that is not possible. The Eye of Balim will destroy you."

"I have to take that chance."

"My friend, make your escape. But take your friends and your boat to Mayran, or to whatever land you may find out there. Do not give up your life for nothing."

"Will you give me the coordinates?"

"Is there nothing I can say to turn you from this rash action?"

"Nothing."

"Very well, I shall provide you with the coordinates. He grasped Masters' hand. "May Balim smile upon your venture."

Masters wasn't too sure he wanted Balim to smile upon him. When Balim smiled, dire things usually happened. However, he knew what Nikto meant.

"Thank you, friend."

*   *   *

The next days were spent in preparation—planning the rescue of Perrin and the others and obtaining special clothing and goggles to be worn during the attempt. Masters had finally told Delia of the captain's presence on The Seeker in order that they may also provide him with the protective clothing, which she promised would be delivered to The Seeker in plenty of time.

And, each evening was spent with Leila. He wished to spend as much time with her as possible before the end. He knew he could not stay, and he refused to jeopardize her life by allowing her to make the attempt with him.

*   *   *

As usual, Iltarn was informed of the Day of Sacrifice. He was surprised that it was to be held on the morrow, several days early. He had checked with his sources in the Temple and learned that D'Ar had chosen one of the otherworlders, the young, dark-haired woman he had seen at the Review, for this day's bloody ritual.

He and Jennifer had become quite close after the Alliance; she had proven herself a true friend and a deserving partner; he truly enjoyed the company of this bright, outgoing girl. They had spent many hours conversing and exchanging information on the culture and mores of each one's world. He was amazed at the scientific progress that had been made in a world that his legends told him was primitive and savage and she, in turn, was appalled at the idea of human sacrifice, which was no longer in her world.

She learned, too, that he did not approve of this practice and was ever seeking some way to sway the people of Encandor away from D'Ar in order to put a stop to the Day of Sacrifice. Thus far, however, he was only able to gain small support in this area, so afraid of D'Ar were his subjects. He would continue until he could break D'Ar's power in the Temple and his extraordinary hold upon the people.

He knew, also, the reasoning behind the gift to him at the Presentation. He had accepted because he did not wish to arouse any suspicion by his refusal of this gift. Better that D'Ar believed that his secret purpose was fulfilled, than to know of Iltarn's plans to thwart him and, perhaps, to depose him altogether.

However, when he learned of this new problem and had told Jennifer, she pleaded with him to act now and to save her friend. Her tears fell freely and his heart went out to her; however, this new situation might work in their favor and he immediately made plans for them to attend the Day of Sacrifice. He would inform D'Ar immediately of his plans to attend the Day of Sacrifice and, believing that the opportunity would most certainly present itself, he would save at least one more person from Balim's blood-thirsty blade.

He was ill-prepared for Jennifer's response to this. She jumped up from her chair and "attacked" him. At least, that was what it seemed to him. In actuality, she simply was expressing her great joy and wanted to hug and kiss him in appreciation for what he was planning to do. When, finally, he realized what she was doing, he responded accordingly. He truly felt a tremendous gratitude to Balim for the gift of this most wonderful creature. He smiled inwardly and wondered if D'Ar was aware of the blessings he has showered upon his enemy.

*   *   *

December 25, …

December 25. Christmas Day. Masters had just come from Antius' apartment where he had dined with him for the last time. Looking forward with anticipation and regret to his last evening with Leila, he entered his quarters to freshen up.

He was surprised to be greeted there by a very angry and irritated Naila.

"Did you really think you could trick me?"

"Trick you? What do you mean?"

"Do you think I do not know what you are planning with my sister?"

"I don't know what you are talking about. I have done what you asked—even though you did not completely keep faith with me, I might add. Even before I agreed to do what you asked, you seized my friends and have them … I don't know where. I do not even know if they are safe."

"Now you lie. My sister has told you they are safe."

"Really? And how would you know that?"

She reddened. In her anger, she had said more than she planned. "Never mind how. I know! What did my sister promise you?"

"What did she promise me for what?" Masters was at a loss to understand what this was all about. He could think of no way Leila could hurt Naila. At least not now. Nor could he remember that they had said anything of their plans in the apartment. What could Naila be talking about?

"I know my sister leads a conspiracy against me and you were supposed to find out who is with her and what they are planning to do. And, now you are in league with her. I would know what she has promised you to betray me."

"Leila? In a conspiracy? Against you? How ridiculous. And that's what you wanted me to discover?" It was a serious situation, but so ludicrous that Masters burst into laughter.

This angered her all the more, and she stormed from the room.

Masters realized that he must contact Leila. He had been worried about putting her into jeopardy on the boat and he had done it right here himself. He could not go to her now, but Antius could get in touch with her. Better not try the communicator here; he would go outside the Temple—and he must hurry. He had not a moment to lose if Leila were to be safe.

*   *   *

A caped and hooded figure slipped along the dock, up the gangway of The Seeker, and stealthily made its way down the stern ladder, through the corridor past the passenger cabins and down to the crew's quarters.

"Davis?" It was hardly more than a whisper.

Knocking on first one door, then another, the figure continued on.

"Davis?" A little louder now.

*   *   *

Davis had been on deck watching, as he had been every night of late. And particularly this night. Masters had been here earlier today and the plans were made for tomorrow. He wanted to make sure that nothing went wrong.

He saw a little movement along the dock. Squinting his eyes to get a better look, he could just make out a figure moving toward The Seeker. He knew someone would be coming, but could not understand why they would have to sneak around. Masters had just walked on board this morning with no problem at all. He did not like this turn of events.

He watched until the figure was about to the gangway, then moved back out of sight. When the figure boarded and started down the ladder, Davis was following at a safe distance. When he saw that the mysterious intruder was going down into the crew's quarters, he lunged forward and grasped the intruder's arm and spun him about.

With the sudden movement, the hood fell back to reveal a profusion of copper curls.

"A girl?" He was incredulous.

"Captain Davis, I believe?"

His mouth slightly open, he merely nodded. She was beautiful.

"I am Leila. I come from Masters. He has sent the clothing as promised and asks that you provide me with suitable quarters." She smiled mischievously. "I am going with you tomorrow. But the soldiers must not see me before it is time."

*   *   *

When Antius had contacted her earlier, Leila had rushed over to see Delia and explained her plan. Now that Naila was suspicious, she was no longer safe in the Temple and where could she go but with Masters? Delia knew Masters' feelings, but agreed that Leila could be no worse off in the Eye of Balim than in the bad graces of Naila. The clothing for the captain had not yet been delivered to The Seeker, so they decided that Leila should be the messenger and then stay on board. It was unlikely that the captain would have much time to chat with Masters the next day before sailing, so Masters probably would not discover her until it was too late to do anything about it.

Before embracing her friend for the last time and leaving for The Seeker, Leila asked Delia to get a message to her personal servant. She must allay any suspicions that might arise at the morning meal. D'Ar's rule was steadfast and he must be advised that she would not appear, else he would send for her, and that must not happen.

She then took her leave of Delia, promising that should they not make it to the other world, but yet survived, she would somehow get word to her.

*   *   *

Masters had paced most of the night away. He had heard nothing from Antius and was unaware of whether or not Leila was safe. Things were not going very smoothly and this was a one-shot deal. There most likely would be no second chance if they missed.

He heard the outside door open and stepped behind the bedroom door. He didn't need any more surprises right now. He heard footsteps cross the room, pause at the bedroom door, then enter. He grabbed the figure from behind. A package fell to the floor.

"Masters! Hold up! It is I, Nikto."

"Nikto, what are you doing here at this hour?"

"I have come to help you. Naila has ordered that you attend the ceremonies tomorrow and has provided you with special clothing. This I have brought—and at this hour so that on the morrow I may report to Naila that you were in your quarters when I delivered them. Now, you must leave and make your final plans for morning.

"I have arranged for the day guards to attend the ceremonies, so the way should be clear for you."

"What about the night guards? They will have to be relieved first. How did you handle that?"

Nikto appeared slightly uncomfortable. "I will relieve the night guards, telling them their relief was held up but a moment and I will watch until they arrive. They will not question my orders.

"I must bid you goodbye now, as I, too, am ordered to attend the ceremonies tomorrow, and will not see you again."

Masters reminded Nikto of the coordinates for The Seeker. "Masters, is there no way I can persuade you to abandon this foolhardy plan? It is sure death."

"It would be easier with the coordinates but, with or without them, I plan to try to go home."

Nikto reluctantly gave him a slip of paper with some figures on it and a floor plan of the Temple. Masters looked at the paper and questioned him about the figures since he could make neither heads nor tails of them.

"I know not how to translate it into your language and can trust no one to do it for me. This is all I can do for you."

Masters nodded his understanding. "Nikto, what will Naila do when she learns of what you have done?"

"Do not worry about that. I will have no problem with Naila. Now, we both must go. You, to your destiny and I, to mine."

It all sounded final and Masters was sorry to lose such a friend for, although Nikto spoke glibly about Naila, Masters did not really believe that Nikto, or anyone else for that matter, could handle Naila, and he feared for his friend.

They left together, but parted in the corridor—Masters to go to Antius and his friends, and Nikto to go to his "destiny."

THE WATCHED AND THE WATCHER

Leaving Masters, Nikto hurried off to complete the plans for tomorrow. He had to pass the observation station on his way, so paused to have ONE LAST LOOK!

*　　*　　*

Tiffany had just expelled one of Naila's servants after getting the news that she was to be the "Guest of Honor" at the following day's Sacrifice to Balim.

The girl was apologetic and Tiffany was sorry she had treated her so roughly. It really was not her fault; she was only doing her duty. However, that did not make Tiffany feel any better about tomorrow's Sacrifice—HERSELF.

She looked once again at the package the girl had left. It contained a costume of multi-colored gems and a very small package labelled TIMSON. Before she was so unceremoniously put out of the women's quarters, the servant girl had explained that, in the morning, she would be here to help and Tiffany was to don the costume, consume the Timson, and await her summons by Naila.

"Await my summons by Naila, indeed." Tiffany ripped the covering off the package and held up the costume. As with the other clothing provided, she was sure it would be a perfect fit but she would "try in on" anyway. It consisted of a type of collar and a skirt which didn't look any too comfortable, considering it was of about a million gems held together by cords and which left absolutely NOTHING to the imagination. Oh, well, what did she have to lose. She stripped off her clothing and put on the costume. Then she picked up the package of TIMSON. She was supposed to wait until morning for this also. The girl had stressed this point more than once. Once again, she thought, she did not have to take orders NOW, did she? What did she have to lose if she did not wait? Only her life. AND, that was going to be taken from her in any event.

*   *   *

This was the first Day of Sacrifice since the otherworlders had arrived and Naila had kept Nikto too busy for him to make any plans for their release or escape as yet. It was his hope that D'Ar would NOT use the otherworlders so soon but it was obvious that Naila had prevailed once again and the tall, dark-haired woman would be the first. Since Naila wanted Masters present, he was sure she believed this girl meant something special to him and was relieved that she had paid no mind to his own objections. Upon arriving at the observation chamber, he dismissed those on duty there. He had locked the door because he did not want to be disturbed during this last observation.

He dialed the women's quarters and searched each room until he found the one he was looking for. He was just in time to see her don the costume and pick up the package of Timson. She opened it. Inside was a tiny vial of an amber-colored liquid. Mentally, he prayed she would not try this also; it was her only protection against the cold blade of tomorrow's sacrifice. It was as though Balim had heard his plea and, in some perverse manner, encouraged the woman to consume it because that's exactly what she did.

*   *   *

Tiffany took the vial from the package and examined it. She wondered what was in it and WHY she should wait until the following morning. Indeed, WHY SHOULD SHE WAIT? Again the same thought invaded her brain: "What do I have to lose?" She could see no way out of this current crisis, and out of a sense of new adventure and not fatalism, she opened the vial and in one big gulp, swallowed the entire contents. There was a hot flash in her throat, down through her chest, and then in her stomach as the liquid made its way down; suddenly and unexpectedly, her entire body was filled with a delicious warmth and she felt as though she were floating. It was as though this TIMSON was consuming her as she had consumed it. At the same time, she heard, or thought she heard, a distant sound of drums. Ever closer and closer, the drums came until she could hear them quite clearly and even make out a sort of cadence or melody. And she wanted to dance.

She started by bending her upper torso forward then while still bending, turning that part of her body so that she was actually gyrating from her waist up, at times bending forward and at times bending backwards. The gems tinkled ever so slightly, adding their sound to the music that only she could hear. The cadence picked up and she followed it beat by beat.

*   *   *

Nikto's eyes were riveted to the screen. He had never seen anything like this before. Apparently, the Timson had quite a different effect on the otherworlders. He was absolutely fascinated; he watched her as she started her little dance and still was rapt as the beat became faster. He could not tear his eyes from the screen.

Then, suddenly, she tore off the collar and threw it aside. She began to caress her breasts quite sensuously in time to the music. And still she danced. The gems in the skirt glittered as the light hit each one in turn and the colors flashed on the wall like a multi-colored kaleidoscope as she continued to turn and gyrate to her own private little symphony. He could see the beads of perspiration appear on her body and glitter in that unearthly light. And he felt a burgeoning in his loins. It was almost more than he could stand and he reached down and stroked himself to relieve the pressure. All the while he continued to watch as she discarded the skirt as well and all that was left was the beading of her perspiration. She suddenly ceased her dancing and looked directly up into the screen he was watching. He was taken aback by this and stepped back from the screen. It was as though she knew he was watching and wanted him to know that she knew.

*   *   *

Tiffany felt that someone was watching her but there was no sound as there was in her dream of the other night. She had felt this "watching" before and she instinctively knew that whoever it was had to be above her since there were no windows or mirrors in the room she was in; however, there was what appeared to be domed lights in the ceiling. She looked directly up but she really could see nothing.

Without further speculation, she continued her dance. The amber liquid was still hot in her veins but she deliberately slowed her pace. If someone WAS watching, she would give them something to watch. She caressed her entire body, using the perspiration as one would use oil and stroked herself in all her delicious places and her dance became more sensual and she became more excited as she continued. She was further titillated because of this "watcher" and her dancing and her caresses became even more sensual than before.

*   *   *

Nikto watched as Tiffany swayed and gyrated, he released the fastener on his pants and his cock seemingly leapt out; he could not remember being so excited before, nor as big, and the thought that this woman was as hot as Naila was cold was almost more than he could stand. Still he waited as the dance proceeded. He stroked his cock, but only gently in spite of his body's insistent demands.

*   *   *

145

The amber liquid and Tiffany's own ministrations were bringing forth an orgasm of quite some magnitude. In spite of that, a lazy thought entered her mind: I really MUST get some more of THAT; it's really great. All thoughts of the next day were dulled and of no consequence at the moment.

Even so, she was not quite ready in her mind when her body, responding to her caresses and the warmth of the Timson in her body, seemed to burst forth in one gigantic orgasm. Her body convulsed slightly and she dropped to her knees and, looking up, she lifted her arms upward for a moment, then bending her head forward and dropping her arms to her side, she simply "melted" onto the floor.

*   *   *

Nikto watched as all this occurred and as Tiffany's dance culminated and she reached her orgasm, he could contain himself no longer and reached his own, his cum spattering on the glass before him.

Still he watched as she dropped to her knees and, looking directly into his eyes, lifted her arms upward as though in a plea for aid. He would never forget the look in those eyes. A moment later, she lay exhausted on the floor below him.

His mind and his body cool once more, he determined that this woman MUST NOT DIE; not tomorrow, not EVER. He must devise a plan to save her. Naila and Balim be damned; there is NO way he would let her die.

ESCAPE

The plans were set. Antius and two others, all known in the Temple, were to accompany Masters to release his friends. Even now they were on their way.

Antius had told Masters that Leila was safe, but that it was not possible for him to see her before he left. It might hinder their plans and, as everything must be done right on schedule, they could take no outside chances.

Antius took them to the rear of the Temple where there was a remote structure, ten feet square and about the same height, containing a single door and no windows. Upon entering, Masters discovered a stairway leading down. They followed the stairway for what seemed ages before it ended in another door, through which there was a long corridor with doors on either side. This corridor struck a chord in Masters' memory. It was like the corridor he was in when he had first met Naila. He wondered if he were in the same area. He consulted the map Nikto had given him of the escape routes from the Temple. It showed nothing to indicate that they were close to the hangar where they first arrived. He caught up with Antius and questioned him about this. Antius showed him on the map where the hangar was located.

"That is not a good route to take, however. There are soldiers in the hangar at all times and it would be difficult to get through undetected."

"But, it's the most direct route. I think we ought to consider it."

"I think it's too dangerous."

"Even though the most dangerous, being the most direct, it would get us to The Seeker faster, and that is our aim now. Time is certainly a major factor."

Antius consulted with his two friends and they gave in to Masters' wishes only after many precious moments of consultation. It was clear they had no wish to tangle with any Temple soldiers.

Without mishap, they reached the quarters where Masters' friends were being held. Nikto had been true to his word—there were no guards. However, when they arrived, they found the door locked and no key that Antius had would open it. He then produced a minuscule model of the weapon Masters had seen on the soldiers when they first arrived. He directed it toward the lock on the door and depressed the handle. A tiny beam of blue light shot forward. There was a red flare as it touched the lock. As quickly as it had come, it disappeared. Antius reached forward and pushed the door open. No one was in sight. Had they been moved?

"Alex! Alex, are you here?"

"Masters, is that you?" The voice had come from behind yet another door. "We're in here."

"Move back away from the door," Antius was already on his way. He had the door open quickly, and the prisoners rushed forward.

Masters quickly explained their plans. He then turned to Antius. "Antius, my friend, it is time for us to part. This is as far as you go."

"You are not out of danger yet. It is my duty to see you safe on board your boat."

"You have done your part. One further favor I would ask. Let me have the weapon and show me how to use it."

Antius hesitated.

"I will not use it except in defense of my life or that of my friends."

Antius complied with his wish and started to leave.

"Wait." It was Sim Barron. "Masters, I'm going to stay and find Helen. I will not leave without her."

Masters glanced an Antius, who merely shook his head.

"Barron, I understand how you feel, but what can you do? The Seeker will be gone. There will be no place for you to go.

You know that if they find you and the rest of us are gone, there will be no hope for you."

"Nonetheless, I must try." He was adamant. "I will NOT leave without her."

Antius stepped forward. "Masters, he can come with us. I don't know if we'll be able to help him solve his problem, but we can keep him safe and try to find a way. Now you must go."

Masters gripped Antius' hand. "Thanks, my friend. Give my love to Leila."

*   *   *

The hangar was quiet. Masters could see no one about. He scanned the distance between the corridor where they were emerging and the outside door of the hangar. There were crates and boxes scattered about. These promised little cover, but it was better than nothing. He glanced down at his watch. He and Delia had computed the time carefully and, according to earth time, they had three and one-half hours to get to The Seeker and get her out to the proper coordinates. Even if they were lucky, they would have only minutes to spare. They started out into the hangar door when the outside door swung open, and two soldiers entered. Masters held up his arm to stop his companions, then motioned to Jack and Skip to follow him. They circled behind the crates in order to come up behind the soldiers—Masters searching for any kind of weapon they might use to incapacitate the soldiers should the need arise. He saw a heavy iron-like bar, which he carefully picked up and handed to Skip as they moved on toward the door.

One of the soldiers had removed his helmet and the two were chatting and ambling along as though they had not a care in the world. Masters motioned to the others to follow, but cautioned against any noise. If they were lucky, they could get through without any problem.

But Fate was not so kind. The trio had almost reached the door, when it swung open and a third soldier entered, hailing his companions. They turned to greet him and one of them saw Masters before he could get behind cover and gave an alarm. Both started forward, drawing their weapons as they came.

Reacting quickly, Jack lunged at the soldier who had just entered, quickly disabling him.

At the same time, Skip rushed forward to meet the other two, swinging the bar as he moved. The bar glanced off the one soldier's helmet, which momentarily stunned him. Before he could recover, Skip was swinging the bar again. This time, he aimed the blow at the base of the skull just below the helmet. There was a ring of metal on metal, then a dull thud as the bar struck home. The soldier was dead before he hit the floor.

The remaining soldier got off a quick shot just as Masters reached him, but his aim was off slightly and Masters felt a searing pain in his left side. He quickly levelled his own weapon and fired, hitting the soldier in the left shoulder, which spun him around slightly and his helmet went flying across the warehouse floor. He recovered quickly, however, and was aiming his weapon again when Masters fired a second shot, catching him in the neck just below his ear. Blood spurted from a cut artery. There was a look of utter surprise on the soldier's face as he dropped his weapon, staggered forward, and slipped and fell in his own blood.

Perrin was rushing forward shouting orders. "Cliff! Skip! Get their weapons and let's get out of here." Perrin reached Masters just as his knees gave way and he crumpled to the floor. "Masters! Are you okay? Here! A couple of you give me a hand."

Two of the crew came forward and helped Masters to his feet. Perrin relieved him of his weapon and led the way out onto the pier. The others followed as quickly as they could, supporting the bleeding Masters. Cliff and Skip brought up the rear.

*   *   *

Leila was in the wheelhouse; she had been watching the pier for the last hour and had seen the soldiers enter the hangar. She now heard a commotion in that direction and saw a group of men come out of the hangar. They were dressed in green. This must be Master's group. She tried to make out which one might be he, but could not tell from this distance.

She waited until they came closer; she must be absolutely sure. Ah, yes. There was the black man. This most certainly was the group. But, where was Masters? She could not find him. Stifling her fears, she fingered the communication button, but was so nervous, her finger slipped off. She tried again.

"Captain, they are here."

Even as she removed her finger from the button, she felt the steady, smooth hum of the engines.

This duty done, she looked again toward the group coming toward The Seeker. She searched again for Masters, but could not find him. She watched until they had reached the gangway and started up before she turned away, tears forming in her eyes. He was not with them. Just as she turned, however, something caught her eye and she looked one more time. She saw two of the men supporting a third. Her heart was in her throat. She looked more closely and, with a little gasp, realized that this third man was Masters. Caution thrown to the wind, she flung open the wheelhouse door, and rushed headlong down the stairs to her wounded lover.

*   *   *

Naila fidgeted with her costume. Twice now she had peeked out into the Great Hall. Masters was not in the assigned place. She paced nervously up and down. Things were not going as she had planned. She had chosen Tiffany to be the Bride of Balim to put Masters in his place, but there was a slight hitch— MASTERS WAS NOT IN HIS PLACE! Just moments ago, she had sent a servant to fetch him, but as yet he had not arrived.

151

And, too, that weak sister of hers had chosen today, of all days, to be ill. She had wanted Leila to witness Masters' humiliation as well.

A messenger arrived at that moment, seeking D'Ar.

"I have a message for the High Priest."

"Give it to me!" Her voice was harsh and strident.

"My command is that the message is for the ears of D'Ar."

"GIVE IT TO ME!"

Still he hesitated. She frowned and started to raise her hand to call the guard. Deciding that the immediate peril was far greater than any assumed peril from D'Ar, he bowed and said, "As you wish, Mistress." He opened a scroll he had been carrying and read:

"D'Ar, Priest of Balim:

"Iltarn, Ruler of Encandor, and Jennifer, Empress of Encandor, will attend the Temple Rites this day."

Naila snatched the scroll from his hand and reread the message. "Oh, Balim!" She spat the oath, and threw the scroll to the floor. What a time for that old fool to pick to visit the Temple—the first time in seven dakars—and he had to pick today. How had he known anyway? She had wheedled her father into the change of dates and was careful to avoid any mention of it other than what was absolutely necessary. She clenched her fists and resumed her pacing, completely oblivious to the messenger and her surroundings.

The messenger carefully retrieved the scroll and went in search of D'Ar. The sooner he got out of Naila's sight the better for him.

"Mistress! Mistress!" Her servant was returning at a run and completely out of breath.

"Yes, yes. What is it?" she asked impatiently as the girl took great gulps of air.

"The tall dark-haired one is not in his quarters and his clothing is still laid out on the bed," she exclaimed excitedly.

Naila swore again and turned angrily to look for Nikto. As she did so, the beads of her skirt made a rustling noise, which angered her even more. Where WAS Nikto? Usually, he was at her elbow. Now, he was nowhere in sight.

She put her fingers to her throat. "Nikto." She muttered his name through clenched teeth. "Attend me at once."

It seemed an eternity before he arrived, though it was only moments.

He bowed slightly. "Mistress."

"Where is Masters? Did I not send you to him at the Morning Chimes?"

He bowed again. "I did as you commanded. He was there when I delivered the clothing with my own hands."

"Well, he's not there now! And he's not here! Find him at once and bring him to me. He must not miss the rites."

Nikto inclined his head in a curt nod and turned to leave. At this moment, however, D'Ar entered the room.

"Where is your sister, Naila? Surely she is no longer indisposed." He turned to Nikto. "Nikto, bring her to the hall for the ceremonies. I desire that she participate today. I have just learned that Iltarn is to attend the rites and everything must be in order."

Nikto glanced at Naila questioningly. She waved him away angrily. This was no time to anger her father. "Bring her and then find Masters."

On his way to Leila's quarters, Nikto thought that things had never before gotten so out of hand. He was glad that Masters had gotten away and wondered just how far they had gotten by now. It was still about an hour until the ceremony. He hoped that things were going as planned. Not so for him, however. Naila was already angry and, as yet, he had seen no opportunity to aid Tiffany.

He knocked lightly on Leila's door.

"Mistress," he called and waited. There was no answer. He knocked again. "Leila, it is I, Nikto."

He heard a rustling inside, then the door slowly opened. Leila's personal servant peeked around the door. "My mistress is ill and cannot leave her bed."

"D'Ar commands her presence in the Temple."

Clearly the girl was distressed, but said nothing.

"Inform your mistress of her father's command." Still she simply stood there.

He was losing patience with this girl. "Did you not hear me? Inform your mistress."

Tears welled up in her eyes. "I cannot."

"You cannot? Why not?"

A single tear traced its way down a satin cheek. "I cannot because my mistress is not here."

The tears were flowing freely now and Nikto was having a hard time learning anything from this girl. He took her hand and led her inside the room where he tried to comfort her and reassure her.

When she finally stopped sobbing, he learned of the message Leila had sent with orders to inform D'Ar of her indisposition. The answer was clear. Leila would not have taken such drastic action were she not with Masters. Why had Masters not mentioned this?

Nikto had completely forgotten the servant and, turning, strode out into the hallway and back toward the Great Hall. Perhaps Masters did not know. Surely he would not risk Leila in such a venture. No, this must have been her own idea. She apparently was more serious about Masters than he had thought. D'Ar was not going to take this news well. And Naila, well…

* * *

AND Naila, indeed! She heard a commotion in the Great Hall.

What now? she thought. The rites had been delayed already because of her sister and Masters. Her father would not like any further delay. She held back the curtain to see what was going on.

At that moment, she heard the trumpets announce Iltarn's arrival. "Oh, Balim." she said under her breath. Could nothing go right? She had planned this day since her very first meeting with Masters and now it was spoiled. And Masters wasn't here yet, either.

She watched silently as the trumpeters entered the Great Hall, followed by several palace guards, then several young girls gaily strewing flowers along the pathway before their emperor and his consort; then another company of guards. Just how much humiliation must she stand? It was bad enough to have Iltarn here; did he have to bring HER with him? She was clearly worried at this new turn of events. Never before had Iltarn attended a Day of Sacrifice. In fact, he had clearly stated many times his absolute disfavor of the practice.

*   *   *

When Nikto arrived at the Great Hall, the procession was ready to begin. He found D'Ar and told him Leila was not in her apartment, mentioning that perhaps her illness was more serious than suspected and she had decided to visit the clinic. D'Ar was obviously displeased, but motioned the procession to begin.

The Flame of Balim would once again be carried by a Temple Virgin. He made a mental note that something must be done about Leila. She had disobeyed his wishes too often, and had not as yet participated in even ONE Day of Sacrifice. This could not go unnoticed by his subjects too much longer and would most assuredly be noticed by Iltarn today.

Naila had chosen one of the strangers to grace the altar today. It was not particularly his desire, but she had cajoled him into granting her wish. He suspected this had something to do with Leila, as did the sacrifice of Kiera. Well, no matter. Soon enough Naila would be making a major portion of the decisions on her own anyway. Her apprenticeship would soon be complete and when that day arrived, he planned to join his beloved Maora. He had honored her wishes and raised her daughters to positions of honor and prestige. Now he longed to be with her once more.

There was a small commotion at the entrance and he glanced that way. The "sacrifice" apparently was not as willing as her predecessor. Two of the Temple Virgins were attempting to escort her into the Great Hall with little success. One of them had a torn gown and the other had lost more than a little of her beautiful hair.

"Hold!" At the sound of D'Ar's voice, all action ceased. The two girls immediately fell to their knees and touched their heads to the floor. Tiffany merely stared, but appeared ready to resume the fight if required.

"Young woman, it is useless to resist. I can have the guard carry you to the altar if that is the way you wish it. Or, I can have you sedated if you prefer. Or, you can get there on your own. The choice of method is yours, but the result is irrevocable."

Realizing the helplessness of the situation, Tiffany relaxed a little. "I will walk. But I would like a moment to myself, if I may?" D'Ar nodded and motioned to the girls to rise and leave. This matter settled, he turned his mind elsewhere.

Nikto watched this little scene, apparently with half interest but his thoughts were in turmoil. He as yet had come up with no viable plan to save Tiffany. To do so, he must put another in her place. An almost impossible premise. Naila had Tiffany moved from the regular quarters sometime late last evening and he had been unable to locate her. Now it was too late to even think of replacing her once the ceremony had begun.

Tiffany had composed herself and now stood at the door of the Great Hall, ready for her entrance, head held high. Naila started her through the door.

This done, she turned toward Nikto. "Have you found Masters?" Even before he could answer, she continued, "Well, DO IT!" She turned with a flourish and, taking her turn in the procession, entered the Great Hall.

At that moment, as Nikto turned to leave and D'Ar moved toward his place in the procession, a soldier rushed into the anteroom, ran directly to D'Ar and prostrated himself at the High Priest's feet, saying over and over "Master! Master!"

Nikto took a deep breath. He recognized him immediately as one of the waterfront guards. Apprehension and concern set his nerves on edge. He moved in closer to hear the story.

D'Ar bade the soldier rise and explain himself.

The soldier rose and said "Master, the prisoners have escaped."

Nikto let go his breath and D'Ar glanced in his direction.

The soldier continued, "They have slain two of the guards and have taken their craft—I know not where."

D'Ar's face clouded over. "Nikto."

Nikto bowed deeply. "I am yours to command."

"Face me!" Nikto looked up. He was none too happy being the object of D'Ar's close scrutiny. Thus far, he had managed very little contact, which was just the way he liked it.

"My place is here." D'Ar gestured toward the Great Hall and the altar. "I place the responsibility on you to seek out and return these prisoners to me. Return not until you have found them."

The words were measured and precise. Nikto understood that should he return without them, his life would be forfeit. He was beginning to rue his involvement in this whole mess. "As you command."

D'Ar was already entering the Great Hall. Nikto stood at the entrance to watch. He had never felt so helpless before. To save Tiffany would be his first choice—even to lose his life but to save her would be acceptable. To leave her to her fate and save his friend Masters and his companions was a poor alternative, but the only one available now. The most he had been able to do was to inform a friend in the Palace Guard of the upcoming events so that perhaps her friend Jennifer might persuade the Emperor to take a hand. The Emperor was here but whether or not he would take action was another matter.

He watched until Tiffany was halfway to the stairs, then turned to obey D'Ar's command.

* * *

Tiffany held her head high and proud as she entered the Great Hall. She realized that her situation was hopeless now, but was determined to meet her destiny with dignity.

She had almost reached the foot of the stairs when she heard a little gasp off to one side and inclined her head in that direction. She saw a strange man dressed in white. Next to him sat Jennifer. She faced forward again and continued walking. She knew if she acknowledged that Jennifer was there, she could not continue on, and there would be no purpose in trying to stop now.

Now she heard Jennifer cry out, "She is my friend. Please do something for her."

Tiffany was well beyond them now and did not see Iltarn motion to some of his guards. They immediately arose and moved out into the aisle. Striding briskly, they overtook Tiffany just as she had started to mount the stairs. One on either side, they took her arms and gently turned her around. She saw that Iltarn had risen and turned to face the audience. "This woman is now in my custody and under my protection, under pain of death."

Tiffany heard these words as though from a great distance as she drifted into the blessed relief of unconsciousness.

* * *

As he turned to go, Nikto heard the commotion in the Great Hall and returned to the door just in time to see Tiffany swoon in the arms of the two palace guards. Nothing could hold him now. He could no longer aid Masters; the Eye of Balim would not open and Masters and his friends could make their way to Mayran without his help. He rushed forward and relieved the two soldiers of their burden. Jennifer was at his side as he carried Tiffany from the hall.

Jennifer caught Nikto's arm. "Where are our friends? Are they okay? Can we see them now? Where are you taking Tiff? Please?"

Nikto had tried to push her away but she was insistent. So many questions…

"They go to Mayran."

"Can she go to them? Please, stop."

He stopped, not because she asked him to but because he thought only to quiet her. He was anxious to care for Tiffany and would be done with this chatterbox. As he turned to face her, a movement in the Hall caught his eye. He was astonished. D'Ar was continuing with the ceremony—WITHOUT A VICTIM? Naila was resisting but D'Ar was insistent and pushed her forward.

He realized suddenly that there was still a chance Masters and his friends might just make it after all. "Come!" He strode quickly away, expecting Jennifer to follow. She had to run to keep up with him but, at the last moment, thought of Iltarn and she turned just in time to see the disappointment and sadness on his face. She made an instant decision and returned to her seat beside him. She took his hand in hers and, leaning toward him, whispered something in his ear. He visibly brightened, then turned his attention to the ritual.

A NEW SACRIFICE

Naila was merely a few steps behind Tiffany and stopped as the palace guards stepped into the aisle. D'Ar continued moving until he reached Naila and gave her a little shove. "The ceremony will continue."

"But…" she started.

"I said, 'The ceremony will continue.'" Again he gave her a little push and propelled her toward the stairs.

Regaining her composure, Naila started up the stairs and took her position at the head of the altar. D'Ar was close behind.

He moved toward the altar and started to mount the two steps. "Father, NO!"

"Naila, you will do what you must."

"Father, I cannot. Not you."

"It is time I joined your mother."

"Father, please, do not ask me. Anyone else, but not you."

D'Ar reached out and took the tray from her hands and placed it on the altar, then took Naila's hands in his own. "Daughter, do not fail me now. This is your moment." When he turned from her, Naila discovered that he had placed the altar key in her hands.

He now looked out over the sea of people in the Great Hall. "I here and now proclaim Naila my successor. Obey her as you have obeyed me. Cherish her and love her as you have cherished and loved me."

D'Ar now mounted the two steps to the altar. He removed his robe, leaving himself clad only in a simple white loin cloth. Leaning against the edge of the altar, he picked up the ceremonial knife and held it high. He turned his eyes upward and cried out, "Maora, I come to you. O, Mighty Balim, my spirit is ready."

He lowered the knife and brought the point to bear just below the rib cage and with a powerful stroke, plunged the knife inward and upward and fell backwards over the altar.

With tear-filled eyes, Naila watched while the two girls straightened the body so that it lay lengthwise on the altar. As though in a trance, she performed the prescribed duties, placing the heart on the silver tray, washing her hands, and moving to the small altar and placing the tray inside.

She glanced back to look at her father once more, only to see that the altar was bare. The body had already been carried below.

Her voice was expressionless as she intoned the words of her father—"Balim, Great God, show us your acceptance of this sacrifice. Let the mighty gales blow; let the waters rise up from their depths—even to the sky; put your lens of darkness over the face of the sun; open your Eye and let your light shine upon our world. Balim, Great God, bring us new offerings for your altar. Balim, Great God, show us your power!"

She turned the key, and as the swirl of multicolored mist rose from the floor and enveloped her, Naila felt the tears start to flow and gave vent to her emotions in great sobs. The one person in the world who had meant anything to her was gone. Her father, D'Ar, the High Priest of Encandor, lay dead on the altar; dead by his own hand.

This was all Leila's fault. Well, she would take care of that little matter. Even now, Nikto was on his way to locate and return Masters and the others who had escaped with him and, when he did, she would show Leila a thing or two. Her grief slowly gave way to anger, then hatred, and by the time the mists had dissipated, so had her tears.

She composed herself and, when the mist cleared, she was once again as an alabaster statue.

With head held high, she started down the steps, avoiding even a glance at the altar where her father had so recently lain. A movement caught her eye and she glanced to her left. There was Iltarn and his consort. This situation was as much his fault as it was her sister's. Her pace quickened as plans for revenge against both Iltarn and Leila began forming in her mind.

*   *   *

Masters roused from a half stupor. He was back in Leila's apartment and she was running her fingers through his hair. He felt her cool hands on his brow. He reached for her. "Aagh." The pain was excruciating. He opened his eyes. Light flooded through the porthole. Memory came quickly … the fight; the flight … he was on board The Seeker. "Leila…?"

"I am here."

"But, how…?"

"Never mind that now. You must rest. The wound is small, but you have lost much blood."

"Are we…?"

"We are on the way. It will not be long now and we will know."

"Leila, I did not want this for you. The danger is so great; the chances of success so small."

She leaned over and kissed him on the forehead. "Know you not that I would die a thousand deaths were I not with you?"

Weakness, combined with the constant hum of the engines, overcame him and he drifted into a half sleep.

*   *   *

Leila heard a commotion on deck and went to the porthole to see if she could learn what was happening, but no one was in sight on that side; all she could see was a vast expanse of water. She glanced at the bed. Masters was still asleep. She slipped quietly through the door, closing it behind her.

Starting up the ladder, she was nearly knocked off balance by a crew member, who pushed past her. She had just stepped on deck when she saw the Temple ship. Her first thought was that her father had found her out and had sent the soldiers. But how could he have known where to look for her. No, it must be something else. Perhaps they had learned of the prisoners' escape. That must be it—she remembered the commotion on the

162

dock and Masters' being injured. It must surely be the guard who turned them in. She breathed a sigh of relief. Her father probably did not know. Then the realization struck her that it did not really matter whom the soldiers were after, or how they found out; when they arrived and took them, she would stand as guilty as the rest.

The ship was drawing closer and she wondered if the plan of escape would be thwarted just when it was so close to fruition. Perhaps the captain would know. Through the confusion on deck, she made her way to the bridgehouse. The captain was peering over some maps and glancing at a small instrument mounted on a little pedestal. He looked quaint in his otherworld clothes. He had flatly refused to put on the protective clothing she had brought. From time to time he would look out first one window, then another.

"Captain Davis, are we going to reach the coordinates in time—before the soldiers reach us, I mean?"

Davis looked at her from bloodshot eyes. "I don't know, little lady, but we're going to give it our best shot." He squinted at his watch. "It's just minutes, and I'm not altogether sure how good a friend that Nikto is of Mr. Masters. And, I don't rightly like to rely too much on strangers for my calculations."

She stood quietly by, watching while he checked and rechecked his instruments. Then he fingered the communications button. "Cut the engines." He turned to Leila. "We are at the coordinates Masters provided. If this doesn't work, it'll not matter too much, as the soldiers will be here in another two or three minutes and…"

His sentence was cut short by a loud roar and both he and Leila were thrown to the floor and held there as though by a great weight. Leila tried to speak, but found it very difficult. Then, suddenly, she felt herself picked up and seemingly was floating in midair. She grabbed for the first thing handy to hold onto. It happened to be the pedestal that held the captain's instrument. The captain was thrown across the room and caught the edge of the instrument board in an effort to steady himself, but to no avail. He fell forward and hit his head on the instrument panel. Now everything was spinning and Leila was getting dizzy. She had to cling to the pedestal with all her strength to keep from being thrown upward and outward. She screamed.

"Captain! Captain!" It was no use—he appeared to be unconscious. She watched in horror as his body was lifted upward and flung through one of the windows. The last thing she saw before she ducked her head to avoid flying glass was the captain's body being buffeted like a straw doll in a giant wind, higher and higher. When she looked up again, he was lost from sight.

As quickly as it had come, the wind abated, and the boat settled slowly and quietly back into the water, from whence it came. Leila looked quickly about. Her heart sank. The Temple ship was still there, though at some distance. They had failed! She was heartsick. As soon as the major motion had stopped, she left the bridgehouse to go below and be with Masters when he learned of their failure and the waiting soldiers.

PHILADELPHIA FREEDOM NEWS
Philadelphia, PA December 26, …
MIRACULOUS RESCUE
Captain of The Seeker Alive

API, Miami, FL

John N. Davis, Captain of The Seeker, a 110-foot yacht belonging to millionaire Alex Perrin, was found today by a Coast Guard helicopter answering a call from a freighter which reported an unidentified object floating in the waters of the North Atlantic about sixty miles Northeast of Puerto Rico. The wreckage found at the scene is presumed to be a part of The Seeker, although no definite markings were found.

An intensive search lasting five days and ending on December 11 was made by the Coast Guard and the Navy, but no trace of The Seeker or survivors was found at that time. A new search for survivors is currently underway.

Davis is in a state of shock and is continually rambling about having hidden below deck and watching some men in strange clothes take his passengers prisoner.

Doctors at County General feel that Davis must have been in the water for several days, shock and exposure accounting for his delusions. The doctors, however, are at a loss to explain the unmistakable odor of whisky on Davis' breath at the time he was found.

Friends have reported that Davis began drinking heavily some two years prior due to an automobile accident in which his wife was crippled. Davis was driving the car at the time.

Some sources, however, since this occurrence was within the mysterious "Devil's Triangle," tend to give some credence to Davis' story. Davis is the first survivor of a mishap in the Devil's Triangle to relate a story of anything other than natural phenomena.

MAYRAN

Leila moaned softly and became restless. She twitched and turned and, finally, awakened. Again, in her mind's eye, she saw the captain being tossed by the wind and blown upward through the Eye of Balim; the boat slowly settling back into the waters of the Lake of Kaos; the Temple ship waiting to take them back to Encandor. She remembered, too, that she was on her way back to Masters when she slipped on the rung of the wheelhouse ladder and fell headlong to the deck.

She now felt a cool hand on her brow and opened her eyes. Who was this strange woman? She was almost sure she had seen her before. She searched her mind, straining to remember but could not.

"Ah, you are awake. Reg will be so happy. He has been quite worried."

"Worried? Why? How is he?" Leila was suddenly aware that she had not reached Masters' cabin.

"My dear, you have been in a coma for several weeks; we were so afraid for you. You had a very nasty fall on the boat."

"Yes. The boat." Her memory was coming back slowly. "You are one of the otherworlders?" It was definitely a question.

"Yes. My name is Helen. My husband and I were brought here a couple weeks ago to be with the rest of the passengers and crew of The Seeker."

"Where is here?"

"Why, Mayran, of course. The boat was brought here by the soldiers after it failed to return to earth."

"It, we, were brought here by the soldiers? I thought they were going to take us back to my father."

"Leila, I don't know how to be gentle with this news; your father is dead. When Tiffany was put under Iltarn's protection, your father offered himself to Balim in her stead."

All this was too much for Leila to assimilate right now. "I want to see Masters. Is he nearby?"

"He will be here shortly. He will be so glad. It has been quite an adventure these last weeks. You rest now. He will see you as soon as he returns."

Satisfied that Masters was okay and close by, Leila closed her eyes and again slept.

* * *

As the boat settled back into the water, Perrin saw the Temple ship and rushed into Masters' quarters. "Reg, Reg, we didn't make it and there is a Temple ship right outside, I guess to take us back to the City. I know you are in bad shape right now, but can you help me? I am a little unsure of how to handle the situation."

Masters opened eyes full of pain. "I guess there is little we can do. If the engines are capable of any power, perhaps we could make it to Mayran; however, if the Temple ship is right outside, I doubt that would be possible." He tried to rise but the effort was too much; he had lost too much blood.

Perrin left him to rest and went back outside. The Temple ship had already arrived. Masters was right. It was too late. Once again, everyone gathered on deck with the exception of Masters, who was still in his cabin, and Leila, who had fallen to the deck and was in the cabin next door. All were crestfallen and quite dejected. Too, there were quite a few of their company missing, notably, Sim Barron and his wife, Helen, Tiffany Crist, Jennifer Craig and especially the Captain, who was lost in the attempted return to earth.

Perrin and the others waited for the ship to navigate as before so they could board; however, it did not. Instead, when the door opened, a single soldier came out and attached a tow-line to The Seeker, then returned to his ship. Perrin called to the others to get below as they were going to be towed—he assumed, of course, to Encandor. A dejected Perrin descended to his stateroom. As he sat down on the bed, putting his hands over his face, he felt a tug on The Seeker. What a deplorable position they were now in; their escape gained them nothing, not even the mainland where, although fraught with danger, they would at least have been afforded some semblance of freedom.

After a short period, he could stand the suspense no longer. He first checked on Masters, who was asleep, then went back up on deck. To his great surprise, they were not going back to Encandor; it was apparent now that they were headed for Mayran. What a relief! But, why? And, who was taking them there?

Just then, the Temple ship stopped; the door in the side opened and Nikto walked through and close behind came Tiffany. What was going on here? Wasn't Tiffany to be sacrificed? AND, without a sacrifice, there would have been no explosion—but there was. He rushed over to the railing and called to Nikto, who turned toward the small craft and waived.

*   *   *

After talking with Nikto, Perrin set about the business of finding a suitable site for living quarters. This became much easier when Antius surreptitiously brought Sim and Helen Barron over from Encandor. It seems that there was a lot of luck involved in getting Helen away from Naila. She had been removed from the women's quarters on the eve of the Day of Sacrifice and put in with the young girls in the service of the Temple and Delia was able to tell Antius who, in turn, told Sim and they were thus able to get her away without any furor while Naila still was in mourning for her father.

Now Perrin and Sim made plans for the future of their charges. They started with finding a suitable and protected building site, though they found that the natives on Mayran (mostly persons who escaped from Encandor) were quite friendly and helpful. Then they drew up some plans and put the building in motion. And, during this time, it was necessary to get some type of medical help for Masters, who was not responding well since he was wounded. Then, too, there was the matter of Leila, who remained in a coma for the first three-plus weeks of their stay on Mayran.

Nikto remained in close contact, though he said he could not leave the ship where it might be found by Naila's soldiers and spies. It was here wherein lay the danger to both Nikto, the soldiers who were loyal to him, and to the passengers and crew of The Seeker. Naila was on the warpath. No one was safe, not even those who served her. Jennifer was able to get messages through but, of course, could not come herself. She suggested that perhaps the women would be safe in the Palace but this idea was not accepted very well by the group. While they missed Jennifer, they knew she was not in harm's way and they had no desire to change her status in this regard.

While they were relatively safe and comfortable, the tiny group was ever watchful for danger from Encandor. Naila had gone on a rampage after her father's death and only lately was there a cessation in the human sacrifices. Jennifer had made one trip to Mayran to see her friends and this particularly to tell them that she was with child; a miracle in itself. She was quite happy with her Alliance and respected and loved Iltarn. Her friends were also happy but prevailed upon her to make no further trips because of the danger.

And, while Masters and Leila were ecstatically happy, their union was not blessed with children. Nikto and Tiffany found their own kind of happiness. Helen had passed away some two years after their arrival on Mayran and Sim had taken a native girl to wife. They had a beautiful little girl with copper-gold curls and they named her Helena in memory of Helen.

Delia, who was feeling pangs of conscience about her last contact with Perrin, managed to visit them. She and Perrin reached a comfortable arrangement whereby she was to visit him once or twice a week when able, while maintaining her position in the Temple, and was thus able to keep the group informed of what was happening in the Temple. After about six months, she learned she was with child and eventually had to desert her position at the Temple or suffer Naila's anger. She and Perrin had a son which they named John in honor of the captain.

The crew members, realizing that there was no returning home, also made homes with the natives. Charley, alone, remained steadfastly true to his wife.

REVENGE

Naila fretted while she waited for Nikto to return with Masters and her sister. This definitely had to be handled once they were returned. As she paced to and fro and schemed in her mind what she would do to her sister, her visage changed from that of sadness to one of sheer evil and raging anger. "Where could Nikto be? He certainly should have found them by now. He MUST return soon."

But, Nikto had not returned. No one had seen him and it had been long since her father had died, sacrificed in place of that otherworlder, and Nikto, her trusted servant, apparently had betrayed her as well as Masters and her sister and had helped them escape.

She had inquired and learned that the only place to which they might have escaped was Mayran, that untamed, savage land. And she had sent her soldiers daily to Mayran in an effort to locate the escapees, all to no avail. Oh, some persons had been sighted a few times, but none had been caught and no one had seen either Leila, Masters, or any of the otherworlders. They had seen the craft of the otherworlders and Nikto's ship once or twice; however, when they returned, neither could be found.

In her anger and frustration, Naila had planned a bloody purge; no one was safe from her wrath. The first to go would be Helen Barron. One more disappointment; the woman was gone and, try as she might, she could find no information on her escape. In her anger, the smallest transgression might merit punishment on the Altar of Balim.

Matters went from bad to worse until, finally, everyone avoided any contact with the Temple and those in Naila's employ. The streets were empty except for messengers hurrying to do their masters' bidding; and not many of those travelled the streets in the daylight hours unless it was an absolute necessity. The Great Hall stood hollow and empty. No one attended the Rite of Sacrifice anymore, even though commanded; indeed, no one attended ANY Temple service. Naila's promises and threats carried little weight these days.

*   *   *

Naila felt her authority slipping away and had called in her closest advisors. It had been almost one dakar from the date of her father's death and they suggested that perhaps a celebration in honor of D'Ar's death might be appropriate and a cessation of human sacrifice might serve to appease the populace. Naila had reluctantly agreed to this plan of action and called for a great feast in honor of D'Ar. All the people of Encandor were invited and a special invitation was sent to Iltarn and his special "guests" from the world on the other side of the sky. The invitation indicated that a special pronouncement would be made, something of great benefit for the people.

The people accepted Naila's invitation and pronouncement of the end of human sacrifice with considerable distrust. But Naila had kept her word and for another full dakar, although sacrifices were made in the Temple, those sacrifices were bloodless. The people of Encandor slowly returned to the Temple and the religion of their past.

Naila frowned now as she looked out over the city. It had been two dakars since D'Ar, as High Priest of Encandor, had made her his successor and then sacrificed himself to Balim on the altar. She remembered Iltarn's interference with the rites— that stupid old fool—had he not chosen that moment to save that woman, the dark-haired stranger who had arrived with Masters and his friends, her father would still be alive. She could still see his body as it lay stretched on the Altar of Balim. Tears welled up in her eyes at the memory. Tears of anger as well as sorrow. Sorrow at the untimely passing of her father; anger that Leila had eluded her all these years; anger that Nikto had betrayed her; anger that Masters, whom she had sought to humiliate and destroy, had escaped and still lived to her own humiliation.

A fresh breeze ruffled the silk curtain and brought with it a light fragrance of flowers. A smile played fleetingly across her face; a hard, cruel smile of self-satisfaction. Revenge had been hers at last! Four days since, Nantu had brought her word that a woman had been captured on the shores of Mayran; a woman with copper curls and the bearing of a priestess. Surely this must be Leila.

Upon receiving the news of the capture, Naila had immediately ordered preparations for a special "Rite of Sacrifice." Nothing and no one could dissuade her from this course of action.

Even when the captive was brought before her and she found herself faced by a young woman of approximately two dakars, she refused to change her mind. She was convinced that this young woman, though certainly not Leila, was the product of a union between Leila and Masters and thus her revenge would be all the sweeter. Denials and protestations by the young woman fell on deaf ears.

No advance notice was given of the nature of the special "Rite of Sacrifice," and those attending were left aghast. There had been much protest afterwards but Naila, sated with blood lust and self-satisfaction, paid no heed to these rumblings, certain only that Leila and Masters were aware by now and beside themselves with grief. She anticipated their actions and ordered her soldiers to keep a close watch on the shores of Mayran in order to effect their capture and make her revenge complete.

EPILOGUE

The swirling waters captured the tiny boat and sucked it downward. Overhead, the sky was black with an occasional flash of lightning. The air was oppressive. Breathing was all but impossible. The waters started closing in over the boat. Young John Davis woke himself with a scream of terror. The sheets and pillow were wet with sweat and stank with the smell of fear.

He opened his eyes to see his father standing over him, a concerned look in his eyes.

"Nightmare again?"

The boy nodded his affirmation. "I don't understand it, Dad. This is the third night in a row. And why now? You told me that story so long ago and we've been coming out here all these years and I've never had this nightmare before. I don't like the feel of it."

"It's just a dream, son, nothing more." He tried to comfort the boy.

John, Jr., almost twenty-five now, nearly a man, was still a boy in some ways. And now, looking down at his son, Davis realized the price of his obsession these past several years and just what he had put the boy through.

Every summer, every school holiday and, after the boy was out of school, almost full time, they had come out here, here in the Devil's Triangle, to search for that Well of Hades; trying to find a passage back to that other world where his friends were trapped.

Well, this had gone on long enough. Fourteen years, and more, of his son's life were enough to pay. He made an instant decision. Tomorrow morning they would return home and that would end the quest forever.

"Come on, son, let's go up on deck and get some fresh air. In the morning, we're going home."

The stars twinkled brightly in the crisp night air. The water looked oily in the faint glow. Young John had never felt closer in spirit to his father than at this moment, looking out over the vast expanse of black water.

Without any warning, a heavy gust of wind caught the sail and threatened to topple the small craft, almost spilling the two men into the water. Before they could fully recover from this near disaster, a blinding light filled the sky. The nightmare was beginning again. But how could this be? He was wide awake. He looked at his father. In the unnatural light, he was white as a ghost, his face frozen in terror. A gigantic wave lifted the boat and tossed it into the air. John reached for his father and held him in a tight embrace as his nightmare became a stark reality.

The boat was tossed from side to side by the capricious dancing of the waves and the two men clung to each other in silent desperation as they watched the sea open up its unholy maw and pull them down into the black abyss of Hell.

So long had Davis prayed for this moment to come and now that it had, he prayed that it would pass leaving them unscathed. Then he cursed his weakness at the thought; he cursed himself for bringing his son to such a sorry pass; and, finally, he cursed God for all the events in his life that passed before him in that last blinding flash of light and his lack of courage in the face of that which he had sought for so many years—so many wasted years. Suddenly, he was very tired and as the tiny craft was sucked down into the vortex, he looked into his son's eyes one last time and slipped quietly into his own final rest.

John had watched in disbelief as his father drifted into that endless slumber but so many things were happening at once that his main concern was survival. The water gave one last tug at the boat, then relinquished its hold, and the boat settled down into an easy, rolling motion and the nightmare ended as quickly as it had begun. John glanced around to see if he could get his bearings but there was nothing in sight but water. There was, however, a stiff breeze coming up from the east and he set the sails. This would bring him home again where he intended to stay; his sailing days were over. He had never REALLY believed that story his father told him anyway and everyone knew about the freak storms in the North Atlantic and he now had to attend to his father's burial and take care of his mother and the rest of the family and ... who was he kidding anyway? This wind WAS NOT going to take him home ever again. As he looked around him at first light, he could see the differences just as his father had described them so many years ago—the sun, the smell in the air, the water.

He must keep busy. First, he must look after his father. He wrapped the body in a tarp, tied it with some rope and attached the anchor (he surmised he probably would not need it anyway), said a few remembered prayers from his childhood and consigned his father's body to the water. Tears flowed freely as he watched it slip slowly from sight. This was as fitting a resting place as any back on earth. What a strange sensation he got from those words "back on earth." Would he ever get back there? Why not? His father had, hadn't he?

He sailed westward the early part of the morning, then the wind shifted and his course changed slightly so that he was now sailing in more of a northwesterly direction. About midday, he sighted land. He remembered what his father had told him but he could see no easy way to overcome the obstacle of ignorance so continued on, sure he had already been spotted from the shore as he was now close enough to see and be seen.

He was coming up on a beach of white sand with a glint of gold; there were a few children playing there and three adults. There was no time like the present to meet the natives—HE HOPED—and he turned his craft toward the shore and beached her. He was committed to this course of action come what may. There was no returning home—this he believed—and so there was no turning back from the course he had chosen.

*   *   *